Finding Home

A Marriage of Convenience Romance

Savanna Golden

ISBN: 979-8-9914457-0-2

First edition 2024

For all the moms out there doing their best to get by. You're doing a great job.

Playlist

Scan to listen.

Note From The Author

This romance is not a dark romance by any means. However, there are a few topics that may be sensitive to readers. Our female main character experienced a toxic relationship with her ex-husband who she divorced. Following the divorce, her children experience abandonment by their father.

Contents

One

Raf

As I walk down the hall toward my father's home office the unnerving silence sends shivers down my spine.

The wood walls of the hallway are mostly shrouded in darkness except for in areas where wall sconces illuminate family photos from over the years. Many of them show a family that is a long-distant memory. Showcasing something we haven't been in a long time. We were a happy family once, but that happiness was fleeting after my mother passed away a decade ago.

Reaching my father's office, I wrap my knuckles against the door, then slowly push it open. He should be aware it's me, he is the one who requested my presence after all.

As I enter, he looks up from some paperwork on his desk. He gives a slight nod in greeting and gestures to the chair across from him.

I hardly ever experience nervousness, I have routines and confidence, but I got called out of my morning meetings to be here, and he didn't say why it was necessary, so that rare emotion is swallowing me, making my suit feel like it's restricting my movements. I remove my jacket and lay it across the back of the chair before taking a seat.

He shuffles the paperwork together and straightens the stack. Picking it up he holds the stack out to me. I glance curiously at his eyes before reaching for the pile.

"What's this about Da?"

"Take a look," he says quietly and waves his hand at the pile again. I guess the only way I'll receive answers is to find them myself.

The more I flip through the papers the more confused I grow. They are detailing his plans for our co-owned baseball team. Namely, he is giving his shares to my brother, Carlos. Hell no, this cannot be allowed to happen.

"What is the meaning of this?" I don't mean to say it so harshly, but the words leave me in a clipped rush. Anger is boiling in me at an alarming rate. He knows that Carlos hasn't been a part of our family in a very long time.

My father and I co-own the professional baseball team, the Triple Twisters. We bought it together after I retired from playing baseball. We built the team from the ground up. My Father was a baseball coach when he was younger, and I was a player until I was injured and couldn't continue. We created the team from scratch, scouted our players ourselves, and built a stadium, this has been our lives. Why would he give it away? And to Carlos of all people.

"No," I say firmly, tossing the stack of paperwork back onto the desk before sitting back, crossing my arms, and glaring at him so he sees how serious I am.

"Look, you know how much I don't enjoy this. The team is everything to the two of us. But I spoke with Dr. Kingsman this morning." Kingsman has been my father's oncologist for the last year. After the brief silence, he takes a deep breath and I know whatever comes next isn't going to be good news, the resigned expression on his face is telling. "He got my latest scans back and unfortunately the treatment isn't working as we hoped. He said that I should get my affairs in order. He thinks I have about six months left of my fight." He says the last part not meeting my eyes as he gazes towards the window.

My heart feels like it dropped to my stomach. My father is the only family I have left. If you want to get technical, I have my younger brother too. But I don't count him. He lives his life separate from us as if we don't exist.

When my father is gone, I'll be alone. Mother is gone already, and work has always been my focus, so I haven't put any effort into building a relationship with a woman that I can share my life with.

"We should get another opinion."

"Son, I know this is not the best news but unfortunately, I've already gotten two other opinions and they all agreed with Dr. Kingsman's prognosis. The treatments are not working, and they all agreed that they think the best thing for me would be to take things easy and start planning for hospice care."

"I don't like it. There has to be something else we can do. Something different we can try. There has to be." I implore him to keep looking for a solution, practically begging.

"I'm sorry but there just isn't. I need you to accept this and start moving forward with me. We only have a short time to get everything sorted for the team. That's why I wanted you to meet with me today. I wanted to tell you about my health update and go over my plans for the team."

"Why are you giving your shares to Carlos?"

I'm sure my voice betrays my bitterness for my father's health revelation and my disdain at the idea of sharing the company with my brother.

"A lot has happened over the years since he became estranged from us; he got married and had two kids. His daughter is seven and his son is five. He has turned things around since the last time we saw or heard from him. He's matured and has a family to support. Also, it would be a good idea for the next generations of Quinns to get involved in the business. I always hoped this would be a multigenerational family-owned team. I never assumed it would be your brother who would bring that change, I always hoped you would settle down and your children would be part of our Triple Twisters family."

What? He wanted me to have a family. He's never said as much. I don't think I've even had a serious relationship since before my mother passed. I've taken a few women out on dates over the years, but I didn't ever feel like any of them clicked, not enough to try and build something lasting. I wouldn't want anything less than what my parents had after growing up watching them be so in love. As a kid, it felt sickening sometimes to see how they interacted, but now as an adult, I know what they had was something really special, something a lot of people never find.

Would that even be something I would want? At one point I thought I would. But all my time is spent on the team. We co-own the team, but I also manage all our operations. I work relentlessly to keep us on top.

After breaking my dumbfounded silence, I respond with the only thing that comes to mind. "I didn't realize you felt that way."

"Your mother was the love of my life; she and you boys were my reason for everything. Nothing would have been worth having without our family. Of course, I would want a life of love for you son. Someone who loves and cares for you, to be there for you in the good times and the bad. To hold your hand as you navigate life."

As we share a late breakfast, brought in by his staff he continues to go over the plans he's put together. My mind keeps wandering back to the idea of a family. Could I have that? The more I think about it the more I like the mental picture that's forming. Maybe it is time.

Two

Jenny

Two Weeks Later

"Hurry up Hux!" I holler over my shoulder as I drag the two overstuffed backpacks through the front door and toss them unceremoniously into the backseat of my car. Every time I look at my car, I feel mixed emotions. It's weird to think seeing a car can cause conflicting emotions but it is the truth.

The car is a hunk of junk from the early 90s that probably should be rotting somewhere in a junkyard rather than transporting a family. Looking at it feels depressing, but it also provides a feeling of relief because, despite the way it looks it does get my children and me from point

A to point B, and it's only broken down a handful of times. I also feel a small amount of pride when I see it too, because it's something I worked for and purchased myself. It's something my ex-husband Carlos never had a hand in.

I slam the door to the backseat and start trekking back across my overgrown jungle of a yard. It's been a few weeks since I've had the time to mow the lawn, I've been juggling too many things. I also can't afford to pay someone else to handle the task. Thankfully tonight the kids are going to their father's house, where they will spend one full week. I will miss them terribly while they are away and I'm not a fan of them being with Carlos, but it isn't my call to make. We agreed on certain arrangements for their care schedule when we finalized our divorce, and they were supposed to go see him. I will just have to put on a brave face for the kids, save the crying for when I get home alone, and keep myself busy. I have a full list of tasks I plan to complete while they are away, so staying busy should be fairly easy.

Before I can climb the crooked front steps of the house both of my children come bounding out, the door slamming closed behind them.

Rae, my oldest, who is seven, walks down the stairs with her nose in a book, not lifting her eyes to see where she is going. Her love of reading is evident in the way she always takes a book with her where she goes.

"Rae baby, eyes up, please. I can't afford to take you to the hospital if you fall down the stairs and get hurt."

She glances up and with a raised eyebrow and with an exasperated huff in my direction proceeds to the car.

My youngest, Huxley, is my wild child. He behaves fearlessly which is sometimes detrimental to his safety. He's always pushing boundaries and attempting daring stunts. Once he's standing in front of me, for the first time he seems uncertain. The expression of worry he wears is so unlike him.

"What's wrong, Hux?"

"Can I stay home with you? Maybe Rae should go by herself to Dad's house."

He breaks our eye contact and starts shuffling his favorite baseball cards. His cards are his most prized possession. I don't know if it's because baseball is his favorite sport or if it's because it was the last present his father gave him before the divorce. But those cards are a comfort item to him, always in his hands, and he wields them like armor when he is going through something.

I squat down to his level and place my hands on his shoulders to offer my comfort. It felt like his words had a hook pierce my heart and it was being tugged out of my chest. I had already been a bit emotional about the kids spending a week away from me, but knowing he was nervous and didn't want to go is intensifying my misery.

"Hey, Hux, it'll be okay. I bet your dad has some fun stuff planned to do with you guys, he has been looking forward to this week. You will have so much fun, you won't even have time to miss me." I add a reassuring smile to try and show him everything would be fine.

His head downturned, still shuffling his cards, he replies softly, "Okay." Then gives a small unsure smile.

On the drive, the kids were relatively quiet compared to their normal rowdy behavior. Their father's house is about a forty-five-minute drive from the small house we rent. When we divorced somehow his lawyer got the house for him, despite our agreement for the kids to primarily live with me. So, the kids and I had to leave behind our beautiful family home and good school district, moving farther away to a run-down two-bedroom that was in the budget for us, extremely low budget.

When Carlos and I had first gotten married I had a thriving photography business. I was usually booked out months in advance. I had a variety of services; my main bread and butter came from photography sessions that businesses used for branding and content creation for their websites and blogs.

When Rae was born, Carlos talked me into the idea that it would be better for me to stay home with her. He didn't like the idea of her having a nanny or going to daycare. To not create the unnecessary stress an argument would have caused, I reluctantly agreed with him. I told him I would stay home for a year and then we could reevaluate our options.

I was never able to convince him that it was a good idea for me to go back to my business and eventually we had Huxley, and he became even more adamant that I needed to remain home with the kids. He said, "*Who better to raise them than their mother? Would you want some stranger raising our kids, when it's supposed to be your job? We don't know those people.*"

So, when we split up, I no longer had a client base to fall back on since all my past clients had replaced me with other photographers or marketing companies to maintain their services. I tried to contact a few but no one needed me or what I could provide.

Due to my gap in work history and being self-employed before that, most places I applied for open positions were hesitant to take a chance on me. It didn't matter that I needed the job and would do whatever was required of me. Every employer saw me as a risk and usually ended up going with someone fresh out of college. It didn't make a whole lot of sense to me, the fresh-out-of-college kids didn't have any work experience but were somehow in higher regard than me because they didn't take years off. It felt like being penalized for being a parent and caregiver.

During an interview I had an employer tell me that they were not going to risk hiring me because they couldn't guarantee that I wouldn't reconcile with my husband and return to being a stay-at-home parent, leaving them in the lurch. I should have reported them to the labor board for their discrimination, but I didn't want to add more reasons to make any potential employers wary of me.

The divorce decree included a small amount of alimony and child support payments for both kids; however, Carlos has never made one payment.

My meager savings hadn't stretched far with no income. Desperation drove me to sign on with a temp agency to get some work even if the positions were undesirable, to try keeping afloat. I'm still struggling to make ends meet so I continue to apply for other permanent positions and keep an eye out for potential clients who I could recruit to start building my business back up.

The kids' silence made this drive feel like it took hours rather than forty-five minutes. We finally pull up to our house, I mean Carlos' house and there are cars everywhere. One of his neighbors must be having a gathering. The crowd of cars made parking difficult, and we ended up having to park further down the cul-de-sac but once we found a parking spot, we unload the few bags from the car and start the walk to their father's place.

Rae does the honors of ringing the doorbell since she is the kid who is the most excited to be here. She was always a daddy's girl and she's probably struggled the most with the split. She was not happy that we wouldn't all live together any longer and didn't want to be away from her father, eventually, she realized it was better to live with me because he's "been too busy" to spend much time with them.

She's pushed the doorbell several times and after about ten minutes of us standing on the porch, I start to look around. There is some noise coming from the backyard, so I tell the kids I think their dad is out back and head that direction.

The closer we get to the backyard the more my *what the fuck* meter starts going off. It wasn't one of Carlos' neighbors having the get-together. When we get close to the back gate you can see tons of people.

"Mom, who are all these people?" Hux asks.

I can tell he feels even more unsettled now that we are here, and he sees the crowd of strangers.

"I'm not sure honey. Let's find your dad and we will see what's going on, okay?" I reply and give him a reassuring squeeze on his hand.

"Stay close to me, please," I tell the kids before grabbing one of each of their hands to keep them close to me as we weave through this mess looking for Carlos.

When we cross the yard, we find him in a lounge chair near the pool and I instantly regret agreeing to bring the kids here. Carlos is lying back in the lounge chair shirtless, only in swim trunks, and on each arm of the chair is a barely dressed woman. He has one hand groping each of the women, one has his hand on her breast squeezing while he groans, and the other has his hand securely connected to her butt.

Rage takes over. Not from seeing him with these women, I did catch him in multiple affairs, so this is nothing new to me, and we aren't together anymore so to each their own. No, the part of this that has me boiling in anger is the fact that he knew the kids were coming over and yet he decided to have this party and put on this ridiculous display.

I storm closer and can't help but yell, "CARLOS!"

The noise has both of his bimbos jumping in surprise, the one he had his hand on her breast almost falls out of the chair with the shock. Carlos jolts up too. He looks surprised as if he didn't expect to see us here. We just spoke on the phone two days ago though, so there is no excuse.

"Jenny, what are you doing here?" He shouts over the music before he turns to the stereo system and stops the music which causes most of the party to turn towards us and tune into our conversation.

"What am I doing here?" I yell back, seething in anger. "I came to drop off the kids. They're supposed to be staying here for a week. Don't you remember that whole conversation we had a few days ago? What the hell is wrong with you?"

"Oh, right. I remember. Hey kids, why don't you go ahead and change into your swimsuits, and you can hop in the pool."

I give him a look that I hope expresses the sentiment of *Are you being serious, asshole.*

But he doesn't seem to care about discussing this more. He turns back to the stereo and turns the music back up. He strolls back to the lounge chair, grabs a glass of bourbon on his way, and settles back in with one of those women whom he tugs down onto his lap.

I can't believe the audacity of this man. Sometimes I can't understand how we were together in the first place, let alone how we stayed together for years. I would wish for a time machine to reverse the decision to date him if it weren't for the two beautiful souls I got out of the ordeal.

The kids start to head towards the house to do as their dad requested, both looking uneasy, but I tug both their hands and bring them to a halt.

"Yeah, that isn't happening, Carlos. The kids are not going to stay here after all."

My declaration makes him angry. Ire is written all over his face.

"What do you mean, Jenny? They are mine for a week. You said so yourself."

I cover Huxley's ears the best I can before responding.

"Are you freaking kidding me? I'm not going to leave the kids here while you have some crowded drinking party. Leaving the kids to be around a bunch of inebriated strangers while you play around with your floozies. Not happening. This isn't something they need exposure to."

The kids and I start walking back toward the yard gate as fast as I can get them to move. I don't want them to be around these people or see this side of their father.

Carlos however jumps from his chair to follow after us. He is more than unhappy with my decision. He's running after us, spewing all kinds of stupid stuff. He has already indulged quite a bit in his drinks tonight, maybe even other things, I know he has been more than willing to do so in the past so I wouldn't be surprised.

"Get your ass back here Jenny! You are not taking the kids. They can stay right here with me. My friends are cool, they will have fun with us. There is no reason for you to take them. That wasn't our agreement."

I keep pushing forward with the kids.

"Don't make me take you back to court and I fight you for full custody! You know my lawyer is a shark and you're flat broke. Who do you think will win?" He says to me with a triumphant and sinister look in his eyes.

I hate this man so much that sometimes I can't help but wish bad things on him. Not for my sake but for the kids. They shouldn't have to see their dad in the disrepair he has been in, and they shouldn't have to feel the rejection that is constantly creeping in every time he says he's too busy to take them, or in this case forgot and threw a rager.

"Go ahead and try to take me to court. I'll be happy to tell them what kind of environment you are trying to expose our children to. I'll make sure my lawyer fights to get you as little access to them as possible."

"You can't take them from me, Jenny! I'm their father— "

"You might have spawned them, but you haven't been a father to them in a long time," I interject, cutting off whatever rant he was going to start.

With us being on the side of the house and the music being loud, the majority of our conversation is fairly private, however sometime during our fight a man in an expensive-looking suit made his way to within earshot of us. I don't know who he is, but he seems to be intently listening to everything we've been saying. What a prick. Doesn't anyone have respect for anyone else's privacy anymore? The divorce was bad enough to go through because my ex used to be a professional baseball player in the majors. The tabloids were all over the story of our split and spreading gossip and photos of his affairs. There were even more side women that I was aware of. It sucked having all that dragged out for public consumption but at least it ended up coming in handy as evidence my lawyer used to give character reference to what kind of man he was during our marriage.

With a last withering glare at Carlos, I start to herd the children towards the front yard so we can get to our car and get away from this nightmare.

"Jenny wait—" Carlos starts to object to my dismissal of him but before he can continue the man in the suit cuts into his path blocking us from sight.

"Carl," the mystery man says gruffly.

I don't hear anything else that is said between the two of them because I use the opportunity of his distraction to continue fleeing the scene of this disaster.

Three

Jenny

The walk back to the car is slower than our walk to the house. Rae is devastated that she isn't going to get the time with her dad. She seemed to understand that I couldn't leave them there with that party going on, but it didn't make her any less heartbroken. The girl misses her father. Her father might be a capital A asshole, but she's just a kid and doesn't know that. No matter how bad Carlos can be sometimes, I would never try to disparage his appearance to the kids. It wouldn't be right. But she still understands that her dad forgot about her. She dries the marks on her cheeks from the tears she cried when she realized she wasn't going to get to stay.

In contrast to Rae, Huxley is fine with the situation. He didn't want to go to his dad's in the first place so he is more than content to go back home tonight.

After our trudge back to the car everyone loads into our junker, and we take off. We only make it to the gates of the subdivision before my car starts overheating and dies, right there at the gates. Sometimes I wonder if I was a terrible person in a different life, did I do something to deserve this type of punishment?

I spent a few minutes looking in the hood to see what was going on— not that I know what I'm doing but it seems like the appropriate next step when your car breaks down.

Both the kids have their windows down and are losing their minds now that we're stuck here in the heat after the situation they just went through. I understand, honestly, it's relatable. I'm about ready to be as broken down as my car. Can I go to bed and sleep for a week? I feel like I need it. Life has been too much of a mess lately no matter how hard I try to do better for my kids. It feels like I'll never get ahead.

I don't know what to do now about my car. It wouldn't start back up which means I would need to get a tow truck, which will be an unexpected expense. We would also need to get a cab or a rideshare back home and with the distance that would cost an exorbitant amount of money. Then of course the cost of a mechanic shop to repair whatever happens to be wrong this time. None of this is going to be helpful to my budget which has already been stretched thin.

I'm bent over the front of the car observing the smoke coming out from somewhere when a large shadow eclipses me. Startled, I jumped and banged my head on the hood that wouldn't prop open all the way because of the broken rod.

I spin towards the shadow and am met with the hazel eyes of the mysterious suit man. Great, just what I need, some extremely attractive stranger witnessing more of my embarrassment. It wasn't enough that he got to be present for my argument with Carlos but now he gets to see me sitting here broken down and looking pathetic.

The stranger gives a soft smile before tentatively murmuring, "Jenny?" Followed by the raising of his eyebrows as he waits for an answer.

I don't know this man and he has some sort of association with Carlos, close enough to him to know he goes by Carl more often than not since he physically resembles his Irish father more than he does his Cuban mother. His knowing Carlos raises red flags that I probably wouldn't have even raised mentally if I just randomly met this man.

"Who's asking?" It's not a strong response especially since this man most likely overheard Carlos say my name but I feel like maybe playing aloof will be better for me. Or so I tell myself.

"My name is Rafael. I'm Carlos' older brother. I know we haven't met before, so I hope you don't feel too uncomfortable with me approaching you and your kids. I haven't seen Carlos in quite a while, and I just needed to communicate some time-sensitive information to him. I was just leaving, and I saw you parked here, and it seemed like you might be having car trouble. Is everything okay?"

I feel slightly less defensive now that I know that I know who this man is. I have heard about Rafael before from Carlos, whenever talk of the family was mentioned he would only say he cut ties with his father and brother years prior and would drop the conversation.

"Oh, hi. Yes, I'm Jenny. Carlos' ex-wife as I'm sure you heard earlier since it appears you witnessed part of our disagreement. I'm not sure what happened to the car, it just started smoking and died. It showed the heat gauge as being too hot. I'll be honest, I know nothing about cars so I'm a bit out of my league here," I say as I give a hopeless shrug.

He approaches the car with a confident swagger and peers inside to assess the situation.

"I think your car overheated. When was the last time you had your car serviced? I think your water pump went out."

"Shit." It's out of my mouth before I can reign it back in. I gave a slightly guilty smile to Rafael.

He just gives a small shrug to show he's not offended by my outburst.

"You'll probably have to get a tow. Do you have anyone to come to get you and the kids?" He asked me.

"Uhh, not really. We live about forty-five minutes from here. The only person I know would be able to get us is our neighbor, but she's at work today. Although, she might be able to leave if I call." I frown at the idea of being an inconvenience to Sara or causing her to lose out on wages to come to get us.

He is quiet for a minute, appearing deep in thought before he speaks again.

"I could take you. It's almost dinner time, there is this delicious pizza place about ten minutes from here. I would be happy to take you and the kids for a bite to eat and I could drop you home after."

It's a generous offer but I don't know if I want to be spending my time with anyone from the Quinn family line.

We talk it over and after a few minutes of me politely declining and him assuring me that it wouldn't be an imposition on him or his plans, I finally acquiesce.

As we walk back toward his vehicle, he pulls a cell phone from the interior pocket of his suit jacket. He brought the phone to his ear and then made arrangements with someone named Mac to come pick up my vehicle. I tried to tell him that it wasn't necessary and that I would set something up for a tow, but he once again insisted.

I get the kids and their backpacks loaded into Rafael's fancy SUV.

"This is Rafael," I say to the kids, "he's going to take us to eat some pizza for dinner and drop us off at our house after."

The kids seem excited about the prospect of pizza for dinner. It happens to be one of their favorite meals and unfortunately, we haven't been able to have it much lately due to the cost.

"You can call me Raf." He says over his shoulders to the kids. "What are your names?"

"Rae." My daughter says quietly. Still a little sulky from being disappointed by her father.

"I'm Huxley, but you can call me Hux!" My son practically shouts at Rafael with enthusiasm. He has experienced an improvement in his mood since leaving Carlos's house.

Over the ten-minute drive to the pizza place, Raf continued to make small talk with my kids. It was nice to see
someone being so attentive to them beside me for a change.
This man just met them, and he was talking with them
with such ease as if they'd always known each other. They
conversed with him more than I've seen them talk with
their father in the last few months.

Pulling his silver SUV into a parking spot when we got
to the restaurant Raf put his car into park and turned off
the ignition.

"This is the place!" He exclaims with robust enthusiasm.

The kids quickly unbuckled their seatbelts, laughing the
entire time as they hopped out of the car and raced each
other to the front door. I don't think I've seen them so
excited in quite a long time. That realization made me
feel pretty low. I tried to make them happy despite our
circumstances, but it felt hard when it all fell to me. I guess
I can put that guilt aside for the time being and focus
on the fact that here in this moment they are happy and
having fun.

Raf and I caught up to the kids at the front door and
he moved forward and held it open for us all to enter. The
kids ran in and immediately found us a table since this was
a seat-yourself establishment. We followed in and sat down
at the table they had chosen.

The restaurant had an older established vibe. The walls were decorated with framed photos of customers and events throughout the years, and some were in black and white. The tables were all covered with red plaid checkered tablecloths topped with plexiglass that probably made it easy to wipe down the tops.

As a photographer, my eyes were instantly drawn to the photos that adorned the walls. I tried to not be rude and tune out Rafael as he was talking through options for ordering and after our order was decided my eyes went back to the photos.

"Mam and Da used to bring Carlos and I here all the time as kids. This shop has been here for as long as I can remember. It's been a staple in the area. I remember coming here with Da after a lot of my little league games to celebrate wins, and sometimes even to cheer up after a brutal loss. It was a big favorite for us."

"Dad has never taken us anywhere cool like this before," Rae told Rafael as she looked at him with a scrutinizing eye.

"He always took us to places that were too fancy and we had to dress up to go. The food was always yucky." Huxley added to the conversation.

I gave them both a little look that I hoped indicated, *not the time for this.*

Rafael took it in stride and said, "I hate stuffy places like those. I'd rather go where it's fun and comfortable."

Both kids seemed to like that.

Our waitress brought our drinks and placed them in front of each of us. She placed Rafael's drink down last, setting it on the table much slower, shooting him the *I'm interested eyes.* She lingered trying to draw attention to herself. He never once looked in her direction, just said a thank you in dismissal. After a few minutes of standing there being ignored, she let out a soundless huff and walked away pouting. For all she knew we were a family, we all had come in here together and the kids chatted comfortably with Rafael, and yet she thought it would be appropriate to try and be flirty with him.

While we waited on our food order Rafael snuck away to the front desk. He didn't say anything before he slipped away so I wasn't sure what exactly he was doing. He was facing away from me so I couldn't see what he was saying to the person there at the desk. He took something from the person and tucked it into his pocket before returning to our table with a smile.

When our giant pepperoni pizza was delivered to our table a man brought it to us rather than our waitress. He informed us that our waitress had to take her break and he would be our server for the remainder of our dinner. The waiter seemed to have an established rapport that made it clear they knew each other. I would never admit it out loud, but I was feeling a slight tinge of happiness about the fact that our flirty waitress would no longer be taking care of us and that I wouldn't have to watch her try and flirt with Raf. He wasn't mine, so I know it was probably wrong to feel like that about someone I had just met but it still made me feel a bit cheapened that she thought it was okay to flirt with him right in front of me.

The pizza here is to die for. The size is huge, and each slice is bigger than my face. Each time a slice is pulled off the pie there is a trail of cheese trailing behind it and delicious grease dripping from it. I'll have to bring the kids here again sometime when I get a little more financial wiggle room.

When we all have eaten our fill and are sitting in contented silence, I assume we will be getting ready to leave. Instead, Rafael stands and pulls something out of his pocket. He then looks to the kids and says, "Hey, I got you each a game card for the arcade. What do you think, are you up for playing a few games while I talk to your mom for a few minutes?"

Both kids jumped from their chairs ecstatic about the opportunity to visit the arcade. They run off to the game area trash talking to each other in equal measure.

"You didn't have to do that," I told him.

"I know. But I thought they would enjoy it and it would give us a few minutes to talk," he replied.

"Okay," I said back when I had no other really good replies because I wasn't quite sure what he would want to talk about.

"Well, I'm sure by our absence that you figured out that Carlos hasn't had any involvement with Da and me in at least the amount of time you were together. Our Mam died about ten years ago and afterward, things quickly became strained among us. I know that Da would like to meet his grandkids sometime if you are okay with it. I don't know if you know much about him, but he has cancer and was recently told he probably only has about six months left."

"I will consider it," I responded. It's hard to feel comfortable saying yes. I'm not sure I want my kids to meet a man I've never met and who will pass away before long. It might seem like a bitch move to be worried about that part but what if my kids become attached and then lose someone else, they love so soon.

"Can I ask you about Carlos and your relationship?"

I figured he would want to know some information about us. I assumed that was part of his ulterior motives for taking the kids and me to dinner tonight.

"You can ask, but I will reserve the right to not answer if I don't want to."

"Fair enough," he chuckles. "My brother can be a bit of a jerk, so my first question is, what'd he do that led to divorcing him? I assume you left him, not the other way around."

That's bold of him to presume. While accurate without knowing us or our relationship together it is curious that he would make that assumption. Carlos tends to be a charmer, and he was a professional ball player in the majors when we got married. I was just the average girl next door when we met. Then it felt like once I became a mom, I became invisible to him. The first few years after each birth were hard. Lacking adequate sleep, and no personal time since I stayed home with the kids, and the kids always stained my clothes with spills. A lot of people felt like Carlos was slumming it with me and deserved a perfect little trophy wife who looked like she was fresh from the salon daily and had a model-thin body. That wasn't me and those standards were unobtainable.

"Honestly it was a combination of things that had built up over the years. First, the heavy partying that caused him to lose his position on his team. They didn't approve of him coming to games hungover and too ill to play. He disappeared for days at a time to go party with other celebrities. He got into heavy drinking, but I heard from a couple of his previous teammates that they were concerned for his health because they saw him snorting drugs at a couple of the parties. When I confronted him about that one, we had a big blowout but at the time he promised he wouldn't do it anymore. The main thing was all the women. He had several affairs during our marriage, but the last one was the catalyst. Usually, he conducted his affairs on his trips away, trying to hide it from me. But the last time was different. I got home with Huxley; we had just dropped Rae off at a friend's house. When we walked inside, he had some model bent over the couch fucking her in our living room. Thankfully Huxley was being a little slow heading into the house, so he didn't witness that. But when I opened the door, they both saw me, he held eye contact with me and just kept going. I didn't deserve the way he treated me and I decided I wouldn't do it anymore."

I truly am over Carlos and have banished any feelings for him but telling that story and being so vulnerable has caused a slight prick of tears to well in my eyes. Turning my head away towards the game area to check on the kids I have to look past Rafael to see them. When my eyes land on him, his hands are on the edge of the table and his knuckles are white from the grip he has. I quickly averted my gaze to the kids. Is he mad that I said all this? Does he think I'm lying?

"Anyways, if you do a news search on the web of your brother, I'm sure you can read all about it. Several newspapers and magazine companies wrote about it during our divorce proceedings. They were able to compile quite the list of women that he had affairs with most of the articles even included photos that people had taken. It was quite a popular story." One that multiplied my humiliation and let the whole world know of the ordeal I went through.

Four

Raf

I t's already been two weeks since the night I met Jenny and that woman is still haunting my mind. When I saw her at my brother's house, I immediately thought she was the most beautiful woman I had ever laid eyes on. She was short, maybe only 5 foot 3 inches tall with a curvy body that was entirely too sexy. Her honey-brown hair was around shoulder length with slight natural waves, and it looked effortlessly beautiful. Freckles ran across the bridge of her nose and dotted her forearms. But the most striking of all were her eyes; they were a shade of brown that almost looked like they glowed. Meeting her only reinforced my opinion that my brother was one stupid motherfucker.

She allowed herself to be vulnerable with me in a way you don't experience often in life. Her story about what happened between her and my brother made me so angry. Knowing the man my brother has become over the years I have no doubt she was truthful, and that was infuriating.

He had built a family with this woman he was supposed to love but instead of nurturing her and his children, he spent his time squandering everything he had. He chose to not be faithful to the goddess of a woman he married and avoided his kids as often as he could.

I one hundred percent believed everything she told me, but I still did a little digging. A very easy web search and I found article after article detailing my brother's infidelity. Most were with models— none of which could hold a torch to Jenny.

Knowing all the shit he put his family through made me even more sour that my father intended to leave his shares of our team to Carlos. He wanted him to take over his ownership to help his family financially and create a legacy for the grandchildren. But there would be no changing my mind that Carlos didn't deserve to be handed the shares from Da and would most likely cause nothing but scandals and ruin for the Triple Twisters.

I've spent this past week trying to figure out what to do about the situation. I needed to find a way to convince

Da that leaving Carlos any of the team shares would be a mistake of epic proportions.

A good friend of mine who is very skilled at digging into people's lives discretely happens to owe me a favor. So, I asked him to do some digging into both Carlos and Jenny.

This morning, I finally received complete files of the information he was able to obtain.

Carlos has woven himself into a pretty tight bind of his making. Excessive drinking, occasional cocaine use, and constantly garnering bad press, all of which led him to lose his position in the majors. Those same things as well as the affairs lost his marriage to Jenny and his kids. Since the divorce, he has taken up gambling and has drained most of his bank accounts.

Mainly what I found about Jenny made me feel worse about how my brother treated her. She works for a temp agency, taking roles in almost any type of placement— everything from food service to manufacturing. The records obtained show she works anywhere from fifty hours or more a week. All the while she is the sole caregiver for Rae and Huxley.

Her finances are destitute despite how hard she works and the financial records indicate my brother hasn't been paying any of the money he owes her. She is providing for the kids solo. Her car is a piece of junk that has a ton of issues according to the mechanic I sent it to and the house I dropped her and the kids off at is in a very rough neighborhood and looks like something that should be condemned. She is trying extremely hard but is feeling the burn caused by single parenthood.

I had important things to do today for my team, but the longer I sat in the silence of my office the stronger desire burns in me to help Jenny. It wasn't just about resolving my brother's shameful behavior; it was something about her. She deserves so much more than this world has given her. Maybe it wasn't me who should help her, but I wanted to, and money is of no consequence to me. With the decision made, I pulled my phone from my pocket and made a call.

It rang twice before it was answered, "Hey man, I just finished checking it out. What do you want me to do?" Mac asks me.

"Whatever needs to be done, do it. Charge all the repairs to my account. I need you to do me a favor though, when it's done and you arrange for her to pick it up, let me know when she plans to get it."

He answered in the affirmative before we ended the call.

After I had arranged for Jenny's car to be taken care of, I went about business as usual. I attended my meetings, spent time going over financial information, and even snuck some time in to watch the team during practice.

Throughout my day though my mind kept going back to Jenny and the issue of my brother. It made me more frustrated as the day went on.

After work, I decided to stop by my Da's house. I had called on my way over to be sure he was feeling up to the company. His terminal illness has been weighing heavy on me, seeing him deteriorate more daily made me sick to my stomach.

Pulling into the circular drive of what has always been our family home I parked and walked through the massive front doors. My Da usually is in one of two places these days, either in his office or in his room resting. Knowing him he was most likely holed up in his office so on instinct I went there first.

As usual, I was right. I opened his office door and saw him sitting at his desk. With his condition I wished he would learn to relax a little, maybe do something for enjoyment once in a while rather than working all the time. That was a wish that I knew would go unfulfilled. If the roles were reversed, I think I would be in the same position.

I helped Da move from the desk to the sitting area of his office. We both took seats in the dark leather wingback chairs around an unlit fireplace. Da pulled out a cigar and lit it before offering me one. Smoking cigars has always been a pastime of his, one I never had much interest in. The smell of the smoke was nostalgic, reminding me of being a small child and spending time with Da while he worked in his study for long hours. I never picked up the habit of enjoying a smoke from time to time like him, but the scent was enjoyable to me.

I walked around my father's chair and once behind him cracked the window of the office. He was in his remaining days so I wouldn't speak out against him having a cigar, but if I could limit his exposure to toxins I would, hence the open window.

We spent about an hour talking about anything and everything. Mostly it revolved around baseball. The business side of things wasn't the topic of conversation, it was more about the sport in general, our team's performance, and the general excitement of the current season. Our team was off to a good start, and we had high hopes for this year's turnout.

As I'm preparing myself to leave my father says something unexpected.

"So, I was talking to my friend Margot earlier and we got to talking about our kids. She has a daughter, Carey, who's about a year younger than you. She is a manager at a finance company that handles investments. She is single and looking to start settling down. I saw a picture and she's really pretty. You would make a good match. Do you think it would be okay for Margot and me to set the two of you up for dinner or something?"

I sputter a little, choking on the sip of tea I just started to swallow when he threw that grenade my way. I hadn't expected that, and honestly wasn't interested, especially with the honey-haired woman currently occupying all my spare thoughts.

We talked the other day about the future and his hopes for me to marry and have a family. I had hoped it was a one-off situation where he was just mentioning it but not expecting me to do anything about it. That assumption was wrong.

"Da–," I start but he cuts me off before I can tell him no.

"Son, I know you haven't been serious about anyone in a long time, but my time is running out. I hate the idea of you being all alone when I'm gone. It hurts to think about it. Please do this for me."

When he is staring at me with those hope-filled eyes it is hard to deny him anything. But the matter is, I wouldn't be able to go out with this Carey woman, not while I have a different one stuck in my head. Before I even fully conclude why, I hear myself tell him, "I'm seeing someone."

"Oh! You didn't say anything. You didn't even mention it the other day when we talked about the future and relationships. Is it serious?"

"Actually yes. It's starting to get pretty serious. I, uh, didn't say anything the other day because she has kids and we've been taking things slowly up until recently." The lie just flows out like water from a leak.

Fuck. Why am I lying? To my dying father about being in a relationship with my brother's ex-wife. This is most likely going to end very badly.

He bolts upright with excitement and claps his hands together, a gleam in his eye that I don't think I've seen in a while. "That's great! Tell me about her."

I shouldn't have lied. I'm not seeing anyone, and haven't even been on a date since who knows when too long by most people's standards. What should I say about my nonexistent girlfriend? There's only one woman on my mind so I dig myself deeper into my hole, telling my father stuff about Jenny, keeping it vague about who she is but telling him things I know and like about her.

I leave his house without ever actually giving him any concrete details about who she is and where we met. Thankfully he was enraptured by falsehoods and too busy listening to ask for specifics.

My car is parked in front of my home but before I get out my phone rings. I pull it from my pocket and see Mac's name on the screen. His calling is a relief. I've been worried about Jenny not having her car. How is she getting to work? Her jobs are always changing as a temp, so she probably doesn't have coworkers she can catch a ride with.

"Hey, what news do you have?"

"I called her earlier," he tells me. "She's coming in on Thursday to pick up the car around noon."

Thursday is only two days away, so that's good. Her being without a car makes me worried. If there was an emergency with the kids, who would she rely on for help?

"Thanks for telling me."

We hang up and I stuff my phone back into my suit pocket. I climb out of the car and start towards the front door. The yard is magazine-worthy; my front garden has been featured in a local magazine, an edition that showcased the best gardens and outdoor spaces in the state. The team I hire to care for it does an excellent job maintaining it. It doesn't matter to me, having the beautiful flower garden is for appearances but I can't stop myself from briefly wondering if Jenny and her kids would like it.

Taking the stairs up to the porch, I stand in front of the two large doors that lead inside. I put my key into one and push it open. Walking into the house, and latching the lock, I'm met with the same thing as always—silence. This has always been my normal so why does tonight feel so much lonelier?

Thursday is finally here, and I had my assistant reschedule all my meetings. I intend to be at Mac's shop when Jenny shows up to retrieve her car. I need to talk to her but it's highly likely that she won't like what I want to discuss or that I'll come across as creepy.

I've spent the last couple of days reflecting on my life. I've never felt like I was missing something before, but the more I've thought about what my father wants for me the more I feel like he might be right. The more right I felt he was the more alone I started to feel.

Then I would think about the fact that I lied to my dying father. I told him I was in a relationship with Jenny and things were getting serious. If I start dating someone, for real, how would I explain that clusterfuck to him? It's hard to fathom how idiotic I was the other night by lying but it could work in my favor.

Yesterday as I was working, I was trying to figure out how to get my dad to change his mind about giving his shares to Carlos. He will do nothing but damage to our team and future empire if he gets his hands on it. I just need my father to see how bad Carlos is and show him why it's such a terrible choice.

When I was plotting my takedown of Carlos, I had a wild idea. It is completely outlandish and is probably a bit diabolical to even attempt but could be my saving grace. Now I just need to convince one stunning goddess to see the good in my scheming. That's the reason I'm now sitting at Mac's garage waiting for Jenny to pick up her car, so I can convince her to help me. Well, that's mostly the reason. I would try to tell myself it's the only reason I'm here, but I would be lying to myself. In reality, I wanted to see her again and make sure she was doing okay.

Five

Jenny

This week has been hard and it's only Thursday. For most people, Thursdays are almost the end of their work week. But I feel like for me the work never stops. The temp agency I received work through was willing to let me pull a lot of hours this week. The company usually keeps their temps at no more than forty hours a week. Over the last year, I've gotten to know my employment specialist, Jan, fairly well. She knows things have been tight for me lately, so she pulled some strings to get me approved for more hours.

Each week for the next three weeks, I will be working three twelve-hour shifts at a local manufacturing plant that processes cheese, as well as taking some evening shifts waiting tables at a popular nightclub. I've worked openings at both locations before for short periods. The fact that I'm already experienced with both businesses is how Jan was able to get approval for my extra hours. Neither position is ideal long term but is both tolerable short term.

The factory job always messes with my sense of smell; the whole place has a suspiciously rotten aroma. The last time I did a rotation there I couldn't stand the thought of consuming dairy for months. The club is probably the better of the two jobs but has a full list of both pros and cons. Some of the positives include the tips usually being great, the customers tend to be laid back, the workers are generally nice people, and the fast pace of the nights makes the hours go by quickly. The drawbacks are things like the late hours, the slightly skimpy outfits, and the occasional handsy drunk customer.

It's been a little stressful to pick up these extra hours, but I know my already sad bank account is going to become even more meager after paying whatever repair fees my car has racked up. Therefore, despite the circumstances, I will be grateful for the opportunities I've received.

The rideshare I splurged on finally pulled up to the garage where my car was taken. This shop is not one I've ever used before so I assumed it would look like your run-of-the-mill grubby mechanic shop. Seeing it in person proved just how wrong that expectation was.

The parking lot is full of high-end luxury vehicles—mostly foreign makes. The building itself is composed of mostly steel and glass, it looks like something that would be featured in an architectural magazine, all sharp edges and radiates sophistication. I double-checked the name and address that Rafael gave me, once I verified it as correct, I stepped out of the car gulping as I headed toward the entrance. This is probably going to be even more expensive than I thought.

The automatic doors slid open as I walked towards them. When I stepped inside, I couldn't help looking around the room with awe. The waiting area is filled with oversized comfortable leather chairs that have customers lounging casually in. The smell of coffee assaulted me coming from a little self-serve station that had a single-serve brew machine, a variety of snacks, and sodas.

Turning back toward my destination I am greeted by an older man who stands behind a large circular desk. He gives me a friendly smile as I approach him. The closer my steps brought me towards him the higher my anxiety seemed to soar. It's been a hard year and the tight funds have caused me more distress emotionally. It felt like being a failure whenever you had to worry about how to pay for things that you can't go without.

"How can I help you today?" The man behind the desk asks while silently observing me.

"Hi, I'm here to pick up my car. Someone named Mac said it would be ready. My name is Jenny."

"Oh yes! I'm Mac. I have your car all fixed up and ready to go. I'll have one of our crew bring it around to the front. We fixed your water pump and a few other things that we saw were getting ready to break down on you as preventative measures."

They did do more stuff. They didn't even run it by me. What did they fix and how much more money was this going to cost me? This was getting more stressful by the minute. Unconscious of the movement I started wringing my hands together, it was a nervous gesture I found myself doing more often recently. Mac was shuffling papers around on his desk. Once he found what he was looking for he brought a sheet of paper and a pen to the top of the desk and set it in front of me.

"Here is a list of the repairs we made to your car. I just need you to sign here and I can get you the keys."

He handed me his pen and turned away to retrieve the keys. I picked up the paper to move it closer to me and saw it was multiple pages. This was bad. Finding the last page, I signed on the line where indicated.

Mac came back and handed me the keys. "Good to go."

Good to go? He still hasn't told me how much this was going to cost.

He grabbed the paperwork I had just signed and started towards a filing cabinet across the room. I just stood there confused, waiting to see what was going to happen next. He slid open one of the cabinet drawers and started putting away the paperwork. Maybe he felt my eyes still on him because while he was bent over filing, he turned his head to look over his shoulder at me and quirked an eyebrow.

"Mac, umm, you haven't told me about the cost yet." My voice comes out meekly. I was finding it kind of difficult to hold emotion back waiting for the devastation I knew this bill would cause. The feelings of shame and embarrassment are only around the corner waiting for me.

"Nothing is owed. You're good to go." He gave what he probably thought was a reassuring smile, but it just made me feel more confused.

"I'm sorry but I don't understand. There were a lot of repairs made to my vehicle. I owe you something because I haven't paid yet."

"Actually," he looked around for a minute before continuing, "your bill was already paid. Rafael Quinn said to fix anything we found wrong with your car and charge it to his account."

My brain was starting to hurt. I only spent a short amount of time with Rafael the day we met, a couple of hours max. We barely know each other. He said he was having the car taken to a mechanic shop he trusted, and I was fine with that. But I never expected him to take care of the bill. I would never expect someone to do something like that for me. The idea of it leaves me feeling slightly dumbfounded and unsettled. Did he do it to be nice or did he do it out of pity?

In my stupor, I'm sure I mumbled something to Mac before taking the keys and silently meandering back outside to locate my car, but I honestly don't remember what I said or if he responded. My ears felt like they were buzzing. It felt like I was in a waking dream. I had anticipated this bill wrecking me and now I find out it was paid for. My world feels off-kilter.

The haze lightened enough by the time I made it to my car that I heard the friendly shout from across the parking lot.

"Hey, Jenny!"

When I turned my head to look in the direction of my name, I saw the man in question. Rafael stood outside his vehicle that he had just been climbing out of. He waved and started jogging in my direction with a bright charming smile on his face. His beaming smile did things to me that it probably shouldn't. My heart was feeling little flutters in response to it. When was the last time anyone seemed so genuinely happy to see me and greeted me with such warmth? Too damn long, that's probably the reason for the flutters, surely it isn't for any other reason. Waving back at him I duck my head down to avoid making googly eyes at the man.

He comes to a stop in front of me, still smiling. I reluctantly take a minute to look him over. Today he is wearing a blue fitted polo with the Triple Twisters baseball team logo on it and a pair of tan khaki pants that cling to his muscular thighs. When my head tilts back towards his face, I see he witnessed me blatantly checking him out. Whoops. A heated blush steals over my cheeks in embarrassment. It is difficult to be in his presence, he is so attractive, and it's been so long since I've felt an attraction of this level to anyone.

Clearing his throat he asks, "Did Mac get you all squared away?"

My head nods as I frantically fling my keys out of my pocket to dangle in the air. Why do I have to act like an awkward idiot at a time like this? Ugh.

"He said it's all done. But when I tried to pay my bill, he said it was already paid. To be more specific he said it was paid by you." I make sure to give him the most suspicious look I can muster before continuing. "Why did you pay for my car to be fixed?"

He had been looking at me until I asked him that. Once the question was out in the open, he seemed to get nervous, almost shy. He looked away from me and a bit of pink tinged his tan face. Is he blushing? It was an unexpected sight, especially from such an attractive man who seemed fairly confident. Honestly, it's pretty cute to witness.

"It's not a big deal." He said in a rough voice. "I just wanted to make sure your car was reliable to keep you and the kids safe."

We barely knew each other. Yet he was finding ways to show me kindness and care that not many have ever offered. He was concerned about the safety of my kids and me. My heart felt that weird little flutter again and my stomach felt like it was doing loops on a rollercoaster. Why did he have to be so sweet?

"You didn't have to do that for me." It comes out quiet.

His eyes soften, "I know, but I wanted to help you."

"Well thank you." My smile was nervous, but I wanted him to know how much I appreciated his concern and help. It was a huge burden off of me to not have that cost hanging over my head.

"Listen, I came here because I knew you would be stopping by to pick up your car. I have a proposal I would like to discuss with you. Would you be up to grabbing some lunch together while we talk about it?"

He was giving me that megawatt smile again, one that was causing a dimple to pop on his cheek. There was a glimmer in his eyes that looked hopeful and also slightly mischievous. It made me all the more curious about what he could want to ask me about. Unfortunately, I don't have time for lunch today so my curiosity will have to wait to be sated. This was just supposed to be a quick stop to pick up my vehicle on my way to work. I've been working the late shift at the nightclub but today I picked up the afternoon shift too because I don't work at the manufacturing plant, and someone called in sick. I didn't want them to be short-staffed when I could use the money so I was working a double shift.

I felt a little guilty telling him I didn't have time to talk since he just paid for my car's repairs, which were probably thousands of dollars, but I had already promised to work extra today and knew no one else could take my place. I explained the situation to him but still felt like I needed to hear whatever he had to say, so I found myself telling him he could come by during my break at the club this evening.

We parted ways with him saying he would meet me tonight. As I drove to work, I found myself thinking about Raf and against my better judgment feeling excited to see him again.

Six

Raf

Patience hasn't come easily the past few hours waiting to see Jenny again and give her my proposal. The proposal is both figurative and literal because of the topic of discussion. I wish we could have discussed this earlier in a quieter, less distracting environment but understanding how busy she is I agreed to meet her at the club.

Due to nerves, I decided to show up a little earlier than planned, deciding that I might need a little liquid courage. It turns out that showing up early works in my favor because it took almost fifteen minutes to locate a parking space and the one I found was several blocks away, so I'll have to walk.

I'm crossing the parking lot towards the building when I see something else, I didn't account for, the fact that there is quite a substantial line formed at the door that's guarded by a big burly bouncer. I resign myself to the fact I'll be here a while and get in the back of the line to wait. Hopefully, I'll be inside in time to meet Jenny for her break. For the time being, I allow myself to eavesdrop on the group in front of me in line. It's not something I normally do, but I'm trying to get control of my emotions.

"I heard she's working tonight." This is said by a guy in a suit who has his tie loosened, hanging limply around his neck. It's a stupid look, he should just lose the tie.

One of his buddies, who is in a polo and khakis groans before replying, "Fuck. Those tits. But you know how I feel about women with kids." The last part is said with a sneer, his face broadcasting his disgust. "But damn call me Daddy because that's one Mom I want to fuck." He barely contains a groan and adjusts his pants.

The loose-tie guy makes a grunt in agreement with the khaki-wearing guy. But the third of their group, a guy who's wearing jeans and a tight black t-shirt, elbows the khaki wearer in the ribs. "Don't talk like that about Jenny. She's really sweet. And the way she looks here—the outfit, the makeup—it's just what her employers require her to wear. She dresses the same as everyone else here, while she supports her kids, not for assholes like you to drool over her. When we get inside, I don't want to see either of you trying to come on to her." He grits his teeth, causing his jaw muscle to clench before turning away from his friends.

Damn, if he didn't say something I was about to, when I heard they were talking about Jenny like that I felt a tide of anger rising. They are lucky he said something because my response was more likely to be a physical one rather than a verbal one.

I'm still eyeballing the group when the bouncer walks back towards me and eyes me head to toe. "Are you Rafael Quinn the baseball player?" He narrows my eyes as he studies my face a little longer.

A small sigh escapes. One of the problems of being a former professional ball player is recognition. Many athletes enjoy fame, but I never have. I'd rather fly under the radar and not end up in tabloids every time I step out of the house. Resigned to the fact that he already recognized me, I responded in the affirmative. "Yep, that's me."

The gruff serious man lights up with a smile that is shocking in its luminosity. He looked so stern before he smiled, now he looks like he won the lottery.

"Wow. Man, this is awesome. I've been such a huge fan of yours since your start when you first got drafted to the majors."

We shake hands and we talk baseball for a few minutes. He told me all his favorite games I've played in, and I talked about the upcoming season for the Triple Twisters.

"What're you doing standing here?" He asked me with a confused look.

"I'm just waiting to get in. I'm meeting someone here."

He gives his head a couple of shakes before he starts walking toward the door and flagging me to follow.

"Come on, you don't need to wait in his line."

I'm tempted to refuse to cut the line, I hate when people use celebrity status to their advantage, but I can't be late to meet Jenny. This is too important to risk.

We pass through the rowdy clubgoers as he takes me to the back. There is a section roped off with burgundy velvet ropes guarded by another bouncer. It's the VIP section and they set me up with a table.

The table is a rounded booth with seats on one side that face the dance floor and has a good view of the whole place.

This area is quieter and calmer than the dance floor and bar area. It still isn't the best location for having this conversation but at least it's not as loud. I texted Jenny to let her know where I would be waiting and to see if she wanted a drink when she showed up. A waitress who has on probably the smallest black dress I've ever seen stops at my table to get my order. After glancing at my watch, I see

I still have about ten minutes until Jenny's break, so I order a bourbon for me and a glass of Moscato for Jenny. Now I just have to wait for her and pray she doesn't throw her drink in my face when I tell her what I want.

Right on time, I see Jenny walk through the entrance to the VIP section with a nod to the bouncer. Even with the description I overheard about her work attire I still wasn't fully prepared for what I saw when she approached. Even with the modest clothes she's worn when I've seen her before I knew she had mouthwatering curves but the black dress she is wearing now is hugging them tight, showcasing her body. Without a second thought, my eyes do a full body sweep of her. She's wearing a skintight black dress that doesn't even come down to mid-thigh, the neckline plunges low, making it easy to see there is no way to wear a bra with it. Her black heels are at least four inches high, and she still looks tiny even with them on. Her honey-brown hair hangs in delicate waves, the top portion twisted up into a messy bun. The waves look so soft, my hands itch to run my fingers through them, but I'll hold off on that for now.

She finally finds me and walks toward my table, her walk slightly harried as she crosses the room. My eyes are still on her, holding her gaze as she approaches but I can feel the eyes on her. She's beautiful, of course, people are going to look, but it makes me feel like I want to hide her somewhere that only I can look upon her. That thought shakes me a little, where is this possessiveness I feel towards her coming from?

She gets to my table and greets me with a warm smile and a very delicate side hug. I gestured to one of the seats before offering her the wine. "I wasn't sure if you would want a drink, so I got a glass of Moscato just in case." She happily accepts the drink with a thank you and takes a seat.

"Thanks for being willing to meet me tonight. I've been working the night shift a lot here, but I picked up the lunch shift today to cover for a co-worker, so it's been a long day. We close around one, so I won't leave tonight until around two. I would have offered to meet in the morning instead, but I work at the cheese factory tomorrow which is a twelve-hour shift. So, my availability is pretty limited right now."

The tone of her voice is timid and reserved, it almost seems like she expects me to be mad at her for not being available. It makes me wonder how my brother treated her regarding the demands he made on her time. Did he treat her badly when he couldn't get his way?

"It's me who is thankful, I appreciate you being willing to meet with me during your break. You're giving up the time you could spend decompressing in order to talk to me." I accompany my gratitude with the most charming smile I can muster, to communicate that I am being genuine and not displeased with her.

"It's no burden. If I didn't meet up with you, I'd be hiding in the back, trying to avoid the leering cooks." She chuckles nervously before darting her eyes away, making me believe she probably didn't mean to admit that portion about the cooks. I heard how those customers talked about her and acted, making me wonder what she encountered in the back, where they're out of the public's view.

"Also, thank you for getting my car taken care of. I picked up extra work to cover the bill, but the cost would still have been a burden to take care of. So, you said you wanted to ask me about something, what's up?"

I take a minute to fortify myself mentally. Lacing my hands, I set them on the table in front of me and silently observed her for a moment before deciding I was ready to begin.

She already knows that my father is dying, so I start by explaining we co-own the Triple Twisters baseball team, then about him wanting to leave his shares to Carlos. Her nostrils subtly flare when she hears that part.

"A big part of his reasoning for giving him the team is because he thinks he's a caring family man. Da thinks Carlos is still married to you and taking care of the kids, he wanted to help provide opportunities for financial stability and a legacy for the kids. But you and I know the truth about the situation and his behaviors."

"So, tell him the truth about us. Tell him he's divorced and not even scraping the bare minimum on parenting."

"Unfortunately, it isn't that easy to fix. I can't let my father give the team to him; he'll drive it into the ground. But Da knows that I don't want Carlos involved. If I were to tell him about you and the kids, he could just think I am trying to discredit my brother for my gain."

She studies me for a few minutes before she finally speaks. "What are you going to do about it?"

This is the part of this conversation that I have been twisted in knots about. Logically she'll either agree or she won't. The worst that can happen is she says no, and potentially thinks I'm a crazy person but I hope she will consider it.

"I have an idea to take care of the situation, and it could be beneficial for both of us." She narrows her eyes and raises one eyebrow urging me to continue. "My father has been trying his best to convince me to settle down, he's been disappointed that I'm unmarried and childless. He's worried about me being all alone after his death because I'm estranged from Carlos and that's the only family, I will have left. It's not a conventional idea but..." I pause for a second to see if she is putting together the pieces of the puzzle I'm trying to lay down. When she is still staring at me expectantly, I continue. "It won't just be enough to say Carlos is single and shirking his parental responsibilities, nor do I think it would be enough for me to just randomly find a potential wife."

"I'm still a little confused, what are you planning?" She asks me with the cutest look of concentration, a small furrow between her brows.

"Well, I have an idea but first please don't throw your drink at me or hit me," I ask her while raising my hands in a surrendering gesture. "I think you and I should get married."

Before I can continue explaining why this could be a good idea or give more details, she cuts me off by yelling. "What!? What are you talking about, are you crazy?"

"Not crazy," I promise her.

She starts to stand but I place my hand gently over hers on the table to get her attention and also give a reassuring touch. "Please Jenny, I know it sounds insane but please at least let me explain how I got to this idea and how it could be good for the both of us before you reject me." I give her my best pleading look.

She sits back down but settles herself slightly farther away than she was before I brought up marriage.

Jenny releases a humorless chuckle, her cheeks and neck a bit red, most likely from anger. "So, when you said you had a proposal for me, you were being literal."

"Pretty much. Is it okay now if I tell you about my idea?"

When she gives me a small nod and meets my eyes again, I continue. "If we get married my father will see me in the light of being the family man he always envisioned, and it will give credibility to the facts we know to be true about Carlos. My dad will have to see things the way they are rather than believing whatever half-cocked story Carlos will ultimately try to sell him. My hope is all this would get him to give me his shares instead. I know you have been busting your ass providing for yourself and the kids and taking care of everyone. Bless single mothers for everything they have to do. If we do this, there are a few ways this could benefit you. My house is in a safer neighborhood and is in the most sought-after school district in the state.

You could stop working yourself to the bone, I would help financially take care of you and the kids while we are married."

I pause for a minute letting her think about the idea before telling her of my expectations. "*If* you say yes, there are a couple of things we need to agree on. Firstly, we need to be convincing, it has to appear real to everyone other than us. We would announce our engagement as soon as possible, then elope in two weeks. We can say the elopement was due to us wanting to include my father in the ceremony which might not be possible if we did a big elaborate wedding. The other important part, agreeing to stay married until my father's passing. He has about six months according to his oncologist. I don't want him to spend that time worrying about me and the future. What do you think?"

Jenny didn't have much time left on break and I didn't want her to rush to a decision, particularly if the answer was no, so I told her to think it over and let me know. Then I put some cash on the table to cover my bill and tip before leaving. When I got to the VIP entrance, I looked back over my shoulder to glance at Jenny. She still hadn't moved from the table yet and was staring unseeing into the distance, deep in concentration. I made my appeal to her, and now all I can do is wait to see whether she will agree to my offer.

That night I laid in bed tossing and turning. Sleep was hard to achieve, too nervous about her answer, and also a little excited by the possibility that maybe she would say yes. At some point when I was lying there restless, I heard a beep from my phone, notifying me that I had received a new text message. My stomach started doing flips when I saw Jenny's name on the screen. Leaning over, I grabbed the phone and unplugged it. Here goes nothing I thought while opening her message.

Jenny: Fine. I'm in.

Seven

Jenny

Outside the sun was shining and today I was getting married. I'm getting ready in a spare room at the house that belongs to Rafael's father—Jack's house. The kids have yet to meet their grandfather but they will today. I met him a few days after Rafael and I agreed to our deal. He is probably in his sixties with red hair that has some blondish-white streaks in some places, showing his age. When I met Jack, I was surprised to hear he had an accent, which I learned from growing up in Boston before moving to the Kansas City area. He was kind and very excited to be welcoming me to his family, even though technically I was already part of his family, Carlos just hid me. We told him we just wanted to have a small low-key wedding and he insisted that we hold the wedding in the garden behind his home.

One side of the spare room had a large full-length mirror hung on the wall which is where I now stood. Seeing as I've already done the extravagant wedding thing and this isn't even *real*, I insisted on something very basic for a dress. I picked out a long white dress that was plain, but the draping still clung tightly to my curves and then hung loosely at the feet. It's a strapless dress with a sweetheart neckline. I think I broke the wedding shop attendant's heart when I told her no lace or beading. She seemed much less enthusiastic after I told her I wanted something simple and plain. She probably saw her commission dwindling before her eyes.

Despite only wearing very light makeup, keeping my face mostly natural, my hair down, and the simple dress I still feel beautiful. The marriage might not be real, but part of me still hopes that Rafael likes how I look today. The idea makes me blush a little. It's so silly to be worried about. We are getting married strictly for an agreement, so no matter whether he finds me attractive or not holds no relevance today, but I still find myself being hopeful.

As I'm staring at myself in the mirror Rae snuck up behind me and wraps her tiny arms around my waist. In the mirror, I can see her little face poking out from behind my hip. "You look so beautiful, Mama."

Before I could tell her thank you, Huxley added his opinion. "Just like a princess. Are you royalty now?" He asked with his head cocked to the side in consideration.

Kids and their imaginations, ha. "Thanks, and no baby, not a real princess. When people get married, the bride usually wears a pretty dress. I bet a lot of people feel like a princess on their wedding days too."

Huxley comes forward and joins Rae in hugging me as well.

I take a minute to soak in the image of us in the mirror. Rae is wearing a beautiful flower girl dress, it's white and long, with flowers sewn into the waistline. Huxley is wearing a charcoal gray suit that looks so cute with his white silk tie. They were both excited to dress up today, they felt special getting to wear their wedding outfits. They've never really had a reason to dress up before, Carlos always made them stay home from any events that required dressing up.

"Let's go let them know we're ready."

Standing in front of the double doors that exit the home and face the garden I give the kids both a breakdown of what they are expected to do. Once I was sure they knew what they needed to do I told Jenson we were ready to start the ceremony.

Since we kept the ceremony small, there's just us, my kids, Jack, Jenson, Chad, and Sara. Jenson and Chad are Rafael's closest friends and also play for the Triple Twisters. Chad is the center fielder and Jenson is the pitcher. Sara has been my neighbor since I moved out on my own. She is in her sixties and has been a godsend for me and my children. As soon as I moved in, she was there trying to get to know me. She knew about me being a single mom and struggling with not having help. Within a few weeks of meeting, she was voluntarily watching the kids for me while I was at work. She has become a grandmotherly figure for my kids.

Jenson and Chad went out to stand with Rafael and then Rae and Huxley walked out together, going down the makeshift aisle. Rae was having a blast throwing the flower petals on the ground as Huxley escorted her down the aisle. When they got to the front they were supposed to go stand to the side on my side of the aisle. Rae did what she was supposed to but Huxley didn't immediately follow, instead, he ran over and threw his small body in

Rafael's direction. Rafael looked shocked but managed to catch Huxley as his arms wrapped around him. When Huxley unwrapped himself from Rafael's legs he continued to his correct place. The unexpected hug seemed to affect Jack considerably, he was smiling broadly and made several quick swipes at his eyes.

With everyone in their proper places, the wedding song started, and Sara handed me the bouquet of white Peonies. She tucked my left arm into the crook of her elbow, and we started forward together. Rafael knew that both my parents were deceased so when we discussed the ceremony, he offered to have either Chad or Jenson walk me down the aisle, but I wanted it to be Sara. She might have only been in my life for a year but during that time she's become like the mother I'd previously lost and I don't know where I would be without her.

We might be faking our relationship but as we approach Rafael, I can see his throat bob on a swallow, as he looks at me in awe. I guess maybe he thought I looked good after all.

Sara took my hand and kissed the top before handing me over to Rafael.

He smiled and looked at me like I was a precious treasure as our minister started the ceremony. We asked for the ceremony to be short and kept fairly basic with standard vows rather than personalized ones. Before I knew it, the vows were over, and the minister was declaring us husband and wife. At that moment I realized there was something really important that we hadn't discussed—the kiss. It's been two weeks since we agreed to get married but besides a quick hug, we haven't had any other physical affection between us. Now I wondered if this kiss sealing our vows would be the cause of everyone discovering our deceit.

I didn't get a lot of time to worry about it before Rafael leaned toward me. He grabbed the back of my head and the next thing I knew he was crashing his mouth to mine. The kiss was anything but timid, it felt like he was claiming me. It felt powerful and passionate and despite it being our first kiss it felt a lot like we have been doing this our whole lives.

There was some cheering from the adults in attendance. Huxley yelled in excitement while Rae made noises of disgust and told us to stop being gross.

We were officially married.

Eight

Jenny

After the ceremony instead of a typical wedding reception, we have a nice catered dinner on the patio with everyone who attended. It's small and to be honest, perfect. We had good conversations and some good laughs. The kids got to meet their grandfather and enjoyed asking him questions about his life. Huxley has always been a big fan of baseball, so he talked everyone's ear off about the sport and was blown away that he got to spend time with Jenson Hannity and Chad Lawrence—two of his favorite pro players. They all were so kind to him and didn't act the least bit bothered by his never-ending questions.

Sara left after dinner because she had to work that evening, but I was really glad she was able to make it to the ceremony. When Chad and Jenson gave their congratulations and took their leave, we decided it was time for us to head out as well. The kids both wanted to stay longer—especially Huxley—but I reminded him we would be coming back again some other time, and he would be able to get to know his grandfather more then. Ultimately what got them both in the car was the excitement to see the new house and they spent the few minutes it took to get there fighting over who got to pick dibs on a bedroom first.

As soon as we arrived both kids bolted from the car at top speed. I don't think I've seen them willingly move that fast in their entire lives.

"Hey, wait for us!" I hollered to them but they either didn't hear me or were too excited. Unfortunately for them, the front door was locked so they ended up having to wait for us anyway. I grin seeing them stuck standing at the door.

When Rafael opens the door, my kids take off running again and I am afraid that they'll leave a steady trail of destruction in their wake. Thankfully when they got to the living room, which was on the other side of the foyer, they came to an abrupt stop. Both kids were marveling at the large living room.

"Wow, Mom look, that's the biggest couch I've ever seen!" Rae said while frantically waving her pointer finger in the direction of a black leather sectional. To be fair, I'm thirty years old and it was probably the biggest couch I've ever seen too. It could probably fit fifteen full-grown men comfortably.

"What's the point of having a big couch though if you don't even have a TV?" Huxley questioned with a deep-rooted sadness. But before I could respond and tell him not to be rude Rafael flipped a switch on the wall and a screen extended down from the ceiling. At that point, both kids were yelling and shouting with enthusiasm and naming off all the things they couldn't wait to watch on the big screen. I could feel Rafael's eyes on me, so I turned my head slightly in his direction, noticing his amused grin I smiled back. He probably made their night by showing them that.

The kids spent several minutes gawking at the giant projector screen, talking animatedly about all the things they wanted to watch and play on it before we were finally able to round them up to continue the tour.

Rafael took us across the house through the kitchen which was stocked with state-of-the-art appliances and walked towards the sliding glass door. The kitchen was something that cooking enthusiasts would die for, it made me wonder if he spent much time there or if he hired a personal chef.

The door was slid open, and Rafael flicked on the outdoor lights. Just outside was a large patio area that had an outdoor dining table with a set of chairs that looked quite comfortable. The patio also had a large hibachi-style grill and a barbeque smoker next to it.

"Mom! We have to eat dinner out here sometime!" Rae shouted as she jumped up and down with excitement. She looked in awe at the plants surrounding the patio. She loved plants, gardening, and spending time outdoors. This is a paradise for her.

Raf hit another switch and the rest of the backyard lit up. He showed the kids over to the large in-ground pool where they professed their plans to swim daily.

We walked a path over to a small building that was separate from the house. The door was opened and lights turned on and we walked inside. It was a home gym that had every type of workout equipment imaginable. There was also a TV set up on one wall with a section that Rafael told me he uses for stretching and yoga. He took up the habit after his recovery from his ACL injury that ended his baseball career. It was a smart TV that you could broadcast from your phone, which he said is how he plays his yoga videos.

The kids were less enthusiastic about the gym, which was not surprising, but they behaved while Rafael showed me around.

Once we went back inside, he took us down the hallway that led away from the kitchen and living area we started in. Then there was a bedroom that Rafael said he converted to an office to be able to do some of his work from home when he could. When he showed this room there were two desks inside instead of just one. He said he wasn't sure if I would need a space to work as well so he installed the second one for me.

The last room in the hall turned out to be a large game room. The kids ran in immediately to check everything out. One side of the room was loaded with old-school arcade-style game machines. He also had an air hockey table, foosball table, and surprisingly a karaoke machine that he told us he uses sometimes with guys from his baseball team. There was a pool table in one corner of the room as well.

"All the bedrooms are upstairs," Rafael told us before he headed up the dark-colored wooden staircase to the top floor of the house.

The first room on the right side is Rae's room. The walls were painted green so light that it was barely notable that it was a color at all. The bed had a dark green bedspread with a canopy of sheer green curtains. There was a walk-in closet with a built-in dresser, and Rae's clothes were already arranged on the racks thanks to the movers Rafael hired.

"The plants! I love it!" Rae exclaimed before rushing around the room investigating all the new plants that Raf purchased for decorating. I know the kids were fighting earlier about picking rooms but it seemed not to matter anymore now that she saw this room custom designed just for her.

Rae loved plants and was always trying to sneak them into our old house despite not having any planters or gardening supplies. She often would try to dig up plants from outside and put them into random containers she used as makeshift planters.

"Thank you!" She yelled as she threw herself at Rafael, hugging his leg tightly while giving the biggest smile I'd seen in a long time. The moment was heartwarming but it was over quickly, it seemed she realized fairly quickly that she was hugging him and she let go and tried to act nonchalant about the whole thing.

The next room on the same side of the hallway turned out to be for Huxley. Once again, the room was already set up with all of Huxley's belongings from the other house. The room was painted in his favorite color, and it was large enough that despite the large number of toys and books there was still plenty of space.

Across the hall from the kids' rooms was the upstairs bathroom.

"Go ahead and get your pajamas on please and then brush your teeth for bed," I instructed the kids.

They groaned for a minute about not wanting to go to bed, no doubt preferring to spend time in the game room or watch TV on the projector but it was already getting late.

There was one door left in the hall. It was easy to assume it was the master bedroom, which means it was Rafael's bedroom. Moving into his home was a necessary step in our arrangement but I never thought about our sleeping arrangements. So far on the tour, I haven't seen any of my stuff. This being the only room left was like a bucket of cold water being thrown at me. The realization dawned that I was going to be sharing a room with Rafael.

He grabbed ahold of my hand and gently led me into the last room.

His bedroom—now ours—was extremely luxurious. I wondered if it had always looked this way or if he had designed it for me, just as he designed the rooms for the kids.

I walked across the dark hardwood floors into the room. The bed was bigger than I knew a bed could be and was covered with a super soft white comforter. There were fluffy white rugs on both sides of the bed with dark-colored wooden nightstands as well.

The walk-in closet was bigger than my bedroom had been at my old house. One side displayed all his clothes and shoes while the other held all my things. Everything was arranged perfectly. I could easily picture a very domestic vision of us both coming in here in the mornings and dressing simultaneously for our days.

There was a master bath attached to the bedroom. The vanity had dual sinks with white and gray marble countertops. I was hoping his house would have a tub, I had missed having one when I lived at the rundown place I was renting before this. There was a stand-up shower and a tub that could probably fit four full-grown adults. I will be utilizing that tub soon.

As I took inventory of where all my bathroom items were Rafael moved into the room with me. "Is there anything you need me to get for you?"

"No, everything is great. Thank you." Truly everything was great, I meant it. He had been so thoughtful in preparing for my family. Since meeting him I was constantly finding myself in awe of his kindness and generosity.

I tucked the kids into bed for the night with a sense of peace. For the first time in over a year, I truly felt like things were going to be okay. Maybe instead of just surviving, we might thrive for a time.

I readied myself for bed and when I exited the master bath, I found Rafael already in the bed. He was sitting against the headboard with an abundance of pillows propping him up. His pajama pants seemed to cling to the muscles in his stretched-out legs as he lay there with his feet crossed.

He gave me a sweet smile as I walked towards the bed.

I climbed into the cocoon of comfort and felt a mess of emotions. The bed was very relaxing to be in, but I hadn't shared a bed with anyone in a long time. The idea of sleeping in the presence of someone new was a little nerve-racking. It didn't help that I was unfairly attracted to the man. I was going to end up laying here thinking things that are borderline inappropriate to be thinking about my fake husband.

Once I was tucked into the blanket, I rolled on my side to face Rafael. He clicked off the lamp on his nightstand, putting us in pitch darkness. I felt him shuffling around getting comfortable.

I couldn't see him but after a minute I felt a light kiss being placed on my head that was accompanied by a raspy, "Goodnight."

My anxiety faded and I found myself easily falling asleep beside my new husband, who I was faking a relationship with. Somehow I felt more secure laying here next to him than I think I ever did with Carl.

Nine

Raf

In the morning, I awake to the sound of birds singing their songs. I don't need to wake up early today as I am off work, so I didn't set an alarm, but usually, I still get up fairly early so I can get my workout in. Last night at bed I decided I would forgo my exercise regimen so I could see what type of routine Jenny has on the weekend. Our marriage might not be *real* in the typical sense, but we'll still spend a lot of time together so I want to get to know her better.

Usually, as soon as I wake, I'm up and off for the day. Straight to whatever tasks need my attention. Today, however, sleep wanes slowly. I don't remember a time that I've ever felt this warm and cozy. It feels like I could sleep all day, something I probably haven't done in decades.

I'm in the middle of a sleepy exhale when I wake up enough to realize why I feel so cozy. There's a warm body with soft skin wrapped around me. My brain takes a minute to register that it's Jenny. But wrenching my eyes open I am still surprised by the sight I'm met with.

Neither of us remained in the spots we went to bed in. We fell asleep on separate sides of the bed, and I awoke with us both in the middle. Generally, I'm a side sleeper but somehow I ended up on my back. Jenny is lying on her side with her head resting in the crook between my jaw and shoulder. One of her arms is tucked under the pillow with the other thrown over my neck. Her top leg is thrown over my left one with the foot tucked under my right one. We are as thoroughly entwined as a tomato plant growing on a trellis.

I have no idea how this happened, but I can say I don't mind the feeling of her warm curves wrapped around me or her soft skin touching my exposed skin. In the back of my mind, I know I should probably pull away from her and untangle us. She was a little nervous to enter our agreement, to begin with, so if she were to wake up with me like this, she would probably feel uneasy about it. Jenny comes off as an independent woman, who is used to relying solely on herself and is also extremely guarded. I am pretty certain she hasn't always been this way. I can occasionally see glimpses of that truth. The fact is my brother destroyed any sense of trust she previously possessed.

After a few more minutes of soaking in her peaceful presence, I decided it was time to make my move to get up. It's going to be quite the task to accomplish if I don't want to wake her—which I don't desire to do. Gently I grab her wrist of the arm on my neck and move it slowly away from me. Once it's lying on her side, I try to survey our legs. I move my right leg, so her foot isn't underneath it anymore. Then I scoot my left leg out from under her. All that remains now is her head on my shoulder. I tilt my body to the side a little, slanting myself towards her—if she woke up now, she would probably think I was trying something untoward, but I'm not—once we're tilted enough for her head to lay on the pillow, I pull away from her. Unwrapping us felt like playing a game of human Jenga and I won the game because she remained peacefully sleeping.

Normally I sleep in just my boxer briefs, but in the interest of not wanting to scare her I slept in the only pair of pajama pants I own—I'll have to remember later to pick up a few more pairs from the store if this is going to be my new normal. This pair was a little too tight.

Walking to the closet I put on a pair of house shoes to wear for my trek downstairs. I'm not sure what the kids do in the mornings or how long to expect them to sleep, so I decided to go downstairs to see if anyone is awake.

When I make it downstairs I notice the house is still silent, so I assume they're still asleep for the time being.

The first thing I did when I made it to the kitchen was put on a pot of coffee. I'm feeling more tired than usual, I wonder if sleeping in late is the cause since it made me deviate from my routine.

I'm leaning against the counter drinking my coffee with cream when I see two sets of eyes peek up from behind the island. I didn't hear the kids, so I assumed they were still sleeping but I guess I was wrong.

They just stay silent watching me like that for a few minutes as I sip a few more times from my cup. I wonder if they think I don't see them silently observing me. Hopefully, they aren't scared. With that thought I give them a cautious smile, trying to show them that I'm not scary or a threat.

"Morning," I say to them keeping that smile.

Hearing my words, they both pop up letting me see them fully. We all stand there for a minute dressed in our pajamas in comfortable silence. In my mind, I think that maybe this should feel awkward, but it doesn't, something about it feels natural seeing these two kids in my home almost as if they have always been here.

Huxley is the first to break the silence by letting out a stream of uncontrollable giggles. He points at my pajama bottoms that have a popular cartoon character all over them. For some reason, he is amused by my apparel.

"What?" I ask him, arching an eyebrow.

"You're an adult." He replies as if that explains every-thing.

"Yes, I am."

"Well, why are you wearing those?" He laughs more.

The pants were a gift from a friend on the team who has a few kids of his own. I decide it's probably best not to explain to him that these are the only pajama pants I own.

"My friend gave them to me for a present. Sometimes I go to his house for breakfast, and I wear them to his house to match his kids when we watch the show together."

He seems both surprised and excited by the idea of me watching cartoons. It makes me wonder if it is something my brother did with him.

"I love that show!" He yells in an excited voice. "I have a pajama set with the same characters on them."

His grin takes up most of his tiny face. I have a feeling I just made some progress toward bonding—with him at least.

"Maybe sometimes we can match our pajamas and watch the show together!" He's jumping up and down at the prospect.

"Absolutely. This is my only pair like this though, so we'll have to wait until next time that they're clean."

He nods his agreement.

I glance towards Rae, who still hasn't spoken yet. Her hair is wild, sticking up everywhere, and her eyes are barely open. Her facial expression appears grumpy, but she hasn't been moody, so I think maybe she just isn't a morning person.

A grumble comes from one of their bellies, but I'm unsure which. Someone is hungry. I imagine if I was a kid, in their current position I might not feel comfortable rummaging around for food at an unfamiliar house, living with someone I hardly know. With Jenny still asleep, I decided it was probably a good idea to feed them.

I start grabbing a few things from the cabinets and laying them on the counter.

"Do you like pancakes?" I ask them.

Both reply in the affirmative, the pancake idea even gets an enthusiastic reply from Rae who looks like she's half asleep.

I send them off to get dressed for the day and wash up while I make the pancakes.

They arrive back at the kitchen in fresh clothes and sit on the stools in front of the island. As I cook, they pepper me with all sorts of questions about myself. I answer every one of them, even when they ask a couple of questions about their dad. We might not have talked in a long time, but Carlos and I are still siblings, and we did grow up together. They tell me their mom doesn't like to talk much about their dad and that he isn't around much anymore. So, I tell them stories of the good things we experienced growing up.

When the plate beside me is loaded with pancakes I turn off the stovetop and start setting the table. The kids are ready to eat right away but I send them on a mission to get the person who is still missing.

"Go grab your mom and we'll eat."

They take off at lightning speed and don't bother trying to be quiet as they run up the stairs. I can hear them thumping into the room. The door crashes against the wall, I probably need to install some of those rubber door stoppers that I've seen at the houses of my friends who have kids, otherwise, my drywall might take a beating.

"Mommy! Mommy, get up!" I hear Huxley chant.

It's followed by Rae. "Breakfast is ready, Mom. We're having pancakes!"

There is a grunt that is unintelligible from down here but I'm sure it came from Jenny. Followed by some shuffling and more grumbled words.

A few minutes later the kids come rushing back into the kitchen dragging Jenny behind them. They each hold one of her arms as they pull her into the room. I think they would have been back sooner but from the look of things she is in no hurry to get here.

A laugh I can't manage to contain slips out as I look at her in all her morning glory. She looks like the grown-up version of Rae. Hair in tangles, sticking up around her head. Eyes barely open. Yawns fell unbidden from her mouth. Sleep lines crease her face.

At my laugh, she turns in my direction and greets me.

"I see where Rae gets her morning personality from." I point out with another chuckle.

It's already around ten o'clock. I haven't slept this late since probably my college days. Jenny on the other hand looks like she is going to fall over from exhaustion at any minute. It makes me wonder if she's normally this tired or if is it because of how hard she's been working this past year.

A small grin appears on her face despite her eyes being closed before she responds to me. "I'm not a morning person." She gestures to herself as if presenting evidence. "Do you have some coffee? I desperately need some caffeine."

I fix her a cup of coffee following her instructions of how she likes it made. Then place it in her hands and bring her to an empty chair on the island. When I have her settled in, I turn back around to grab the syrup and the pancakes while Rae helps by handing out the plates and Huxley passes around the forks. We work together like a well-oiled machine, getting everything ready to enjoy breakfast together.

We spent breakfast chatting and making plans for the day. After Jenny's second cup of coffee, she seems livelier. Today Huxley has a baseball game scheduled for the little league team he plays on through the city parks board. He practically begged me to attend his game which was unnecessary to win me over; I have no plans today and I liked the idea of going with them.

Once we all have had our fill of pancakes Jenny sends the kids off to collect their stuff while we work together to clear off the counter and put the kitchen back to right.

"Thank you," Jenny says to me. She doesn't elaborate on what she is thanking me for, but I have a feeling it's for more than just a thanks for the breakfast. Maybe it's the breakfast, but I think it's more for taking an interest in the kids, for agreeing to go to the game, maybe for making them feel welcome here.

She excuses herself to get ready for the day and I linger in the kitchen to allow her the privacy of our room. I genuinely enjoyed the time I spent this morning with Jenny and her kids. It makes me realize that I'm looking forward to having more time like this together.

The drive wouldn't have been bad if we had left a little earlier. We ended up arriving at the sports complex with only a few minutes until the team started warmups.

Despite the traffic, the car ride wasn't horrible. Rae went back to napping as soon as her butt hit the seat. Jenny rested against the window and looked inclined to do the same. Huxley, however, had other plans. He regaled me the entire trip with stories of his baseball prowess, going over all his big wins and some of his disappointing losses.

He humbly made it clear to me that he was the best player on the team but made sure I knew not to say anything about it in front of the other players because he said his mother said it was impolite.

When we get closer to the field his team will play on, Huxley takes off towards some of his friends and they all scurry off at a fast pace with excitement.

Rae takes a small blanket out of Jenny's arms and lays it down under the shade of a tree before plopping down on it. If I were to bet, I would probably win some money guessing that she is going to be sleeping before long. I make a mental note to myself to keep an eye on her. A sleeping kid seems like an easy target for a kidnapping victim, and that's not going to happen on my watch.

Jenny and I take seats in the small bleachers. There aren't many seats, but the parents fill it almost to capacity.

Once we are seated several heads turn in our direction and before long, I've been introduced to several of the other players' parents.

Jenny might not have noticed the look on some of their faces when she introduced me as her husband, but I sure did. A few of the men looked like someone was murdering small animals despite their obligatory congratulations on our nuptials.

Once the game was started the talking died down and was replaced by shouts and cheers.

The team ended up winning by a landslide and Huxley truly was a phenomenal player for his age. He was the leading player for tagging opponents out. As well as contributing several runs to their score. He was also a runner for a player who was injured and could only bat. During the game, even during some of the stressful parts, he remained encouraging and supportive of his teammates.

We celebrated the win with ice cream on the way home.

Ten

Jenny

The kids were quietly tearing into their breakfast in the kitchen. A warm cup of coffee, which was probably more creamer than coffee, would be my breakfast. The caffeine was necessary if I was going to be a functioning adult. During these past few weeks of being married to Rafael, I'd had better sleep than I could remember having in the past few years. But the tension between us felt like it was reaching a boiling point.

We didn't fight—it wasn't that kind of tension. We got along great. He was kind, and thoughtful, and always found ways to include the kids and me in his daily life. It felt like we were any other married couple except for the fact that we were faking it. Every night we would lay down to sleep, in the same bed. It was a very domestic feeling, the intimacy of sleeping next to someone every night.

Occasionally I would wake up finding that we had become intertwined in our sleep, on those mornings I would either pretend to sleep a little longer so I could feel the comfort his body gave to mine, or I would sneakily pull myself from the bed before he could wake up. The accidental cuddles were as far as our intimacy went in private. In public, we were very outwardly affectionate, as would be expected of a newly wedded couple. But sometimes I longed for that same affection when it wasn't for show.

I wanted the feeling of his arms around me. Wanted his hand on my lower back or wrapped around my hand. I wanted the sweet kisses. I wanted them to be just for me, just because he cared. I knew that wasn't part of the deal though. But sometimes it was hard to remind myself of that when it felt so natural. I would find myself longing for something that wasn't even real.

Sometimes I even wanted more than those sweet touches. Quite a few times I witnessed that muscular body in action, either in the gym or pool. Sometimes I saw him coming out of the master bathroom shirtless with his chest still slightly damp from the waterfall shower head. Sometimes when a drop of the water would slide down his chest, I would fantasize about trailing my tongue down his taught skin following in the wet wake, the fantasy alone would leave me flustered.

It's been a long time since I had sex, even longer since I had an orgasm that didn't come from a vibrator or my hand. I was starting to feel desperate for release. More often than not finding myself thinking of all the places and positions I would want him to fuck me, dominating my small frame with his larger one. My trusty vibe friend hadn't seen a lot of use recently because it was hard to find time alone to do it, since we were together so much, but I think tonight it needs to make an appearance, even if it has to take place while I take my nightly shower.

"Mom, are you listening?" Huxley shouted at me, stirring me from my lustful fantasies.

"Sorry, I'm still tired. What did you say?" I asked him while feeling a little guilty that I had been ignoring my kid while daydreaming about my "husband".

As if my thoughts had summoned him, Rafael took that moment to appear in the doorway. He came into the kitchen and grabbed an ice-cold bottle of water from the fridge. He was drenched in sweat; it was soaking through his t-shirt. I imagined he was just getting in from using the state-of-the-art backyard gym. This wasn't helping my lust-addled thoughts stay on the straight and narrow.

Huxley started replying to me and I had to shake myself out of my stupor so I could pay attention to my kid.

"I was asking what we were going to do today."

We've mostly been doing the same thing every day. The kids were enjoying spending the day playing in the pool while I would sit poolside in a lounge chair trying to rebuild my empire. I would be laid back with my laptop hunting down leads and going through all the hoops required of small businesses for successful operation.

"Probably just hanging around the house again. Or maybe we could visit the library this afternoon if you want?"

Before I could finish posing the question his little nose wrinkled in disgust. I tried hard to encourage reading, but Huxley still wasn't a huge fan of it. Rae could completely read multiple chapter books in a week, but Huxley treated reading like a dirty chore he had no interest in.

He was loudly complaining about that and insisting on being fine around the house when Rafael cut in.

"The Triple Twisters have a home game tonight. Do you guys want to go? You can sit in the owner's box with me and see some super-secret team stuff." He stage whispered the last part behind his hand while looking at Huxley, whose face broke out with excitement.

Which was how we found ourselves at the home game that night surrounded by lots of recognizable and important people. I had to give the kids a pep talk before we left the house, a pep talk reminding them to be on their best behavior. In my experience, that request would most likely be ignored, if attempted at all. Cue mom's anxiety.

On the car ride to the stadium, Huxley talked Raf's ear off about baseball. Rafael was surprised to find out that Huxley had never attended a professional game before. I could see the questioning glance he sent my way about that. With Huxley's father being a professional ball player and being such a huge baseball fan, it was something most people would probably be surprised to learn about. The truth was that Carlos never wanted us at his games. At the time it felt easier to go along with his controlling demands, let him act as if it was to keep us safe from any potential crazy fans, etc. But really, it would be hard to chase tail with your wife and kids in attendance. Another one of the many times I let him gaslight me. Never again would I stand for his or any other man's bullshit.

When we made it to the stadium, we were able to bypass the crowds and go in an employee entrance thanks to Rafael. Many of the workers we passed greeted him with friendly faces and he knew every person by name and frequently stopped to make small talk. Watching him interact with all of them created warmth in my chest and a smile to grace my face unbidden. It was hard to fathom how Rafael and Carlos were raised in the same household but turned out so differently.

We made it to Rafael's box and stayed there for a bit. The room was enclosed with one side being a full glass window facing the field. The air conditioning made the room much more comfortable than it had been outside. One side of the room was lined with tables covered in all different types of food.

Rafael said there would be food so tonight in preparation I decided to hold off on making dinner. The kids and I ate our fill of the offered delicacies.

Rafael hadn't eaten anything yet; he had been ambushed with conversations since entering the room. My stomach was full and happy. Skipping dinner seemed like a good idea, but now seeing how busy Raf has been I was concerned about whether he would get time to sneak a bite to eat. I watched for a few minutes more and when it seemed like there was not going to be an end to his current discussion anytime soon, I moved back toward the food tables again.

Grabbing one of the larger plates off the stack I surveyed the options again. We haven't been married for long but in the time, I've known him I've gotten to know a lot of the things he likes, so I was feeling fairly confident in choosing items for him.

Having finished filling the plate I moved towards Rafael. I gathered a variety for him to munch on, options for being snacky or for more filling things. There was stuff like his favorite chips, mini weenies, baked beans, some sort of casserole, and some veggie sticks with dip.

He was still talking to the men around him, but his gaze lingered on me as my legs ate up the space between us. His megawatt smile beamed in my direction when I got close.

The men he was surrounded by seemed to notice the shift of his attention. Pausing their conversation multiple heads turned in my direction almost simultaneously. Shoot, maybe this was a bad idea. Nerves started to take over. Before it could get out of hand, he crossed the group to me and put an arm around my waist. He pulled me to him and put a kiss on my cheek before greeting me.

His pleasant welcoming of me helped me feel more at ease with interrupting. I held the plate up toward him, "You haven't eaten yet and I just thought you might be hungry."

That smile kicked up a notch at my thoughtfulness. "Thanks, babe." He took the plate before saying, "This is my wife, Jenny."

My panties practically melted at the tone in which he said "My wife". It wasn't the phrase, it was the possessive way in which he said it. Seemed like even in public surrounded by people my wanton libido had no chill.

His introduction was met with greetings from all the men and congratulations on our new marriage. After a couple of minutes, he said, "It's been great to catch up with you all and I hope it won't offend anyone, but I must be going. We came for a family night with the kids, so I better get them down to the seats before the first pitch gets thrown."

Surprisingly no one seemed bothered by him ending their discussion and after a few well wishes, he snagged my hand before we collected the kids.

He held my hand in one of his and Huxley's hand on his other side, leading us out of the room and down toward some seats that had been roped off.

Eleven

Jenny

This morning, I was up much earlier than normal. I had spent the night feeling restless, lying in bed next to a man who was supposed to be my fake husband but who was starting to feel more and more like a real husband. It was hard to lay next to him and try to remember to keep the lines firmly drawn between us rather than let them get hazier and hazier.

As I lay there unable to sleep, surrounded by his deliciously masculine scent I knew I had to get out of that bed before I let my mind run away with the possibilities of what could be.

I was situated on a stool at the island in the kitchen with a piping hot cup of coffee in one hand while I was working on editing some photos, I took the other night at the baseball game.

It not only surprised me that Raf invited us to the game, but it also made me happy. After we left the fancy room with all the important people, he took us to his special reserved seats. We ate hot dogs and cotton candy just like any other family enjoying a night at the ballpark. The kids had so much fun laughing at all the shenanigans of the mascot that took place throughout the game and amped up as the night went on.

When we were leaving the kids had been so tired out from all the excitement. Huxley insisted his legs were much too tired to walk back to the car. Without any prompting, Rafael scooped him up and planted him on top of his shoulders. Huxley's laughter at being so high up above the crowd was infectious. I got a great photo of the two of them. It's been a long time since I had seen Huxley look so happy.

Just as I was bringing the mug back toward my mouth for another sip a noise behind me startled me. My hand holding the cup jerked involuntarily at being caught un-aware and unfortunately coffee spilled over the lip of the mug at my movement. Some of the hot liquid landed on my hand and it freaking hurt but not bad enough to cause injury. The rest that spilled landed on the counter in front of my laptop, with a couple of drops on the touchpad.

Jumping up quickly I flung my hand back and for shaking off the hot coffee. I quickly crossed to the sink and ran some cool water over the affected skin.

Rafael, who was the cause of the noise that startled me quickly ran across the kitchen space to grab a hand towel from the stove bar before coming to the island and helping clean the mess.

"Sorry! I didn't mean to sneak up on you," he said to me as he was wiping up the mess.

His hands ceased motion as he stared at my open screen. I knew what image he was looking at. The one I was working on last was an image I snuck down to the front row to capture at the start of the game. It was of the opening pitch being thrown, the ball frozen in motion, the pitcher's arm extended from just releasing the ball. The man's face in an intimidating scowl.

I wasn't sure how he felt about the picture until he finally spoke, "Jenny, this is a great photo. Can I see what else you took at the game?"

The majority of the photos I took were already edited with only a few left to process so I went ahead and agreed. I went and brought up the rest of them and watched as he silently flipped through the photos.

"When you ran your photography business did you ever do sports photos?"

"No, I mostly did stuff for branding stuff for small businesses. Portraits and content for them to use for the websites and socials. Stuff like that."

He hummed in response before turning to face me. He looked at me for a long minute, almost like he was sizing me up even though I didn't know the reason behind it.

"We could use something like this for the Triple Twisters. A lot of this would be great for posting on our fan accounts and the photo of the opening pitch is magazine quality. Would you be interested in doing some sports photography for our team? I could set it up with HR to get a contract arranged."

He said it with such sincerity that I knew he meant that he wanted me to do this. I hadn't done sports before, but a lot of the stuff would be similar except actual games. It wasn't quite what I planned but it would get me back into doing what I loved, so I said that I was interested in learning more.

Twelve

Jenny

In the silence of the room, I stare into the mirror in front of me, taking in my features, trying to decide if I look acceptable for what's to come. My brown hair is tousled in soft waves and my brown eyes are lined with slight winged black liner. I didn't cover my face with foundation like I normally do when doing a full face of makeup because Rafael has pointed out several times that he thinks my freckles are beautiful. It's always been something I've been insecure about, but I believe Raf when he tells me they enhance my natural beauty. My lips have a slightly pink tint from the gloss I applied.

A knock at the door had me halting the inspection of my appearance and looking over my shoulder toward the bedroom door. Just as it opened Rafael stepped into the room looking stunning in a form-fitting charcoal suit.

"The guys just got here, are you ready to head out?" His eyes swept over me as I stood from the vanity and walked towards him.

"Yep, all ready to go. What do you think?" I asked him as I gave an excited twirl showing off my floor-length gown which swirled around my legs with the movement. The red dress was silky and contoured to my curves to accentuate my figure before flaring out at the bottom. There were very few times in my life that I wore something as luxurious and well-fitting. I felt sexy, something I hadn't felt in a very long time.

His throat bobbed on a deep swallow before he responded to my question. "You look beautiful Jenny—" Whatever else he was going to say was cut short by a yell coming from downstairs telling us to hurry up. It sounded like it was Jenson who had been the perpetrator rather than the more mellow Chad.

Without waiting further, I wrapped my hand around his arm and headed toward the door. He didn't say anything as he followed me out of the room and down the stairs.

When we started to descend to the first floor Jenson who was obviously in a playful mood tonight started catcalling us, whooping and hollering about how striking we looked tonight. I wasn't used to this sort of attention, so my cheeks flooded with heat at the praise.

Chad greeted me in a tone that belied his amusement at their friend's behavior. Jenson who was still not done with his show grabbed my hand and spun me around in a move I've only seen dancers do before reeling me in for a hug. I froze at the overt familiarity of his actions, but it wasn't long before Raf pulled me out of Jenson's clutches. His words to his friend were friendly enough but the possessive way he held his arm around my waist showed his true feelings. Chad chuckled when he witnessed the move that Jenson was still oblivious to.

This evening, we were attending a fundraiser event that would have the majority of the Triple Twister's players and upper management present. I've gotten to know a lot of them over the last few weeks since starting to work as a photographer with their creative team.

Before leaving we said goodnight to the kids who were staying home with Sara watching them. Even though we didn't live next door to her anymore she was more than happy to stay involved in our lives. The kids were excited to give her a tour of the house when she first got here. Enthusiastically showing off all their favorite things about the house and their new rooms.

Huxley practically tackled Rafael as he threw himself at him for a hug. It warmed my heart to see how close the two of them had grown, he hasn't often had a male to be close with or look up to. But it made me a little nervous too because I didn't want him to be damaged by this arrangement, I didn't want him to be crushed when this was all over.

The party had been much more fun than I originally had anticipated when we discussed our attendance. I was worried it would be stuffy and I would have to stand around pretending to make small talk with strangers who thought they were better than me but that couldn't have been further from the truth.

We spent the time with a core group for most of the night. Rafael's close friends and their dates. I got to meet some of the player's wives, and they were all so welcoming and kind.

The fundraiser ended up raising a substantial amount of money for a charity that works with our local hospitals to help children who are undergoing health challenges.

Unbeknownst to me, Raf's mother used to be involved with the charity as a volunteer before her death, so it meant a lot to him to attend and donate to the cause.

By the time we got back home, the children were tucked away in their beds, and Sara told me all the fun things that they had done together before she headed home for the night. I tried to convince her to stay the night since it was already late, but she wouldn't hear of it.

My feet ached from the height of the heals I wore this evening so after gathering my pajamas I headed to the master bathroom to get a bath. The idea of soaking in scalding hot water sounded divine, the perfect way to end the night. Well, only one thing would make it more perfect, that thought had me snagging my vibrator from its hiding spot before shutting the door.

I turned on the hot water until there was steam rising in the air. Pouring some of my favorite Epsom salt soaks into the water created some bubbles and caused the smell of eucalyptus to permeate the air.

It took a minute to get myself fully submerged as I acclimated to the temperature but once I was fully in the tub a soft sigh escaped my lips. My muscles started to unclench as I relaxed. It wasn't a stressful night, but my body was on edge from standing so close and pretending to be full of newlywed bliss. It was the things I didn't have to pretend that were problematic, mainly my attraction to Rafael. Spending so much time touching him, wrapped in his arms, and laughing with him made me want him even more. It wasn't safe to want him that way, hence the vibrator being my good friend.

I went through the motions of cleaning my body and washing my hair before I succumbed to the intensity of my desire. Reaching over I snagged the vibrator from the small stand by the tub and turned it on. I laid my head back on the edge of the tub, feet propped up on the other side as I brought the device to my throbbing clit.

As I gently glide it back and forth where I ached most, I started to imagine instead that it was Rafael touching me. I conjured an image of him naked, his bronze muscles on display for me as he whispered dirty words in my ear and he rubbed my clit with his callused fingers.

I was lost in my mind enjoying my fantasy when I whimpered, "Raf please," wanting more from the imagined version of him. But directly after my whispered plea, a shocked gasp came from near the door. My eyes instantly flew open in a panic.

Standing there was Rafael. He was shirtless wearing a pair of gray sweatpants and looking completely frozen in motion at what he just witnessed.

Embarrassment took over, I dropped the vibrator down into the tub water and started to stammer out an apology to him. But before I could finish saying how sorry I was he woke from his momentary stupor. He strode in my direction with fire in his eyes.

As he squatted down at the side of the tub, I happened to catch a glance of the bulge of an erection his sweats couldn't hide.

I was unsure what was going to happen, so it was surprising to me when his arm plunged into the tub. He grabbed the vibrator firmly in his hand and maintained eye contact with me as he brought it back to my needy center.

"Raf—" I tried to say something to him, but my words were lost in pleasure as he continued to rub it back and forth against me.

"That's it, wife, come for me." He commanded me.

An orgasm exploded out of me with much more intensity than if I were the one using the device, probably because this was the hottest moment of my life.

When I was starting to come down from the high of pleasure, he scooped me out of the tub and wrapped me in a thick fluffy towel. He plopped me into the bed before covering me with blankets. I thought maybe things were going to escalate, maybe he would want some sort of reciprocation, but he just snuggled behind me and told me to go to sleep.

I wasn't sure if I was glad things didn't go further or disappointed. I laid there, his warm body cocooning my naked one, trying to mull it over when sleep snuck up on me.

Thirteen

Raf

The clicking of my turn signal is the only sound in the car as I turn into the school parking lot. Both Huxley and Rae remain quiet in the backseat. While we've spent time together, we haven't spent much time *alone* together. Mostly we have Jenny as a buffer but not this morning.

I swiftly maneuver into a parking space, and we all get out of the car. Rae seems ready to bolt as soon as she gets her backpack on. I'm not sure why she is acting skittish. Huxley on the other hand seems ecstatic that I'm here and grabs my hand to lead me into the school.

This morning was one of the days we all ate breakfast together. A meal I cooked, because I know Jenny is averse to mornings. She stumbled down the hallway, clad in pajamas this morning grumbling as she ushered the kids to the kitchen just as I turned off the stove top. I'd put together a spread of Belgian waffles, some scrambled eggs, and sliced fruit. I had a steaming cup of fresh coffee prepared and waiting for her.

Everything was going the way it normally does as we ate our breakfast until Huxley mentioned the event today at his school. School started two weeks ago and it's still unclear how the kids are settling into their new school.

Rae seems to be adjusting just fine to the new school. Every evening, she talks at length about her new friends, her teacher, and what she learned that day. Huxley on the other hand, seems to be struggling a bit more with the adjustment. He hasn't said anything directly about not liking the school or kids being mean. But he also doesn't seem overly enthusiastic about it. We've tried to coax it out of him but he always just says everything is fine. Jenny has traded emails with his teacher a couple of times, but she has said that Huxley is doing well in class and seems to be acclimating nicely.

With the better school district came an increase in parental involvement. Jenny said at the old school she only met the teachers at the open house before school started. This one asks parents to volunteer as a 'classroom parent' at least once a month, which involves coming in and helping the teacher and doing projects with the kids. They've also thrown a Mom's Morning, which was a breakfast where the students brought their moms in to eat muffins with them and meet other parents, etc.

At breakfast, Huxley reminded us that today is an event called Dad's Day. They encouraged all the students in his grade to invite their fathers to school for donuts this morning. Huxley has been looking forward to the event. According to Jenny, he has called my brother several times to invite him to come to the school today, but Carlos didn't answer any of the calls and hasn't responded to any of the voicemails.

Huxley gazed at Jenny with excitement when he asked her if his dad was coming this morning. Of course, since Carlos didn't answer we know he won't be there. But it hurt to watch as Jenny tried to explain that she didn't think his Daddy could make it and offered to let him arrive late to school so he didn't have to sit through the event alone.

After quite a few tears shed by Huxley and Jenny both, he turned to me with big sad eyes and asked if I would attend with him. And because I would never be able to say no to that sweet face and the chance to cheer him up, I agreed.

Once we cross the parking lot, Rae races down the hallway toward her classroom. No goodbyes for Huxley and me.

Huxley, who is still holding firm to my hand, looks up at me with a small smile but I can practically see the nervous energy coming off of him. Trying to comfort him, I smile back, giving his tiny hand a quick squeeze.

"Which way do we need to go?" I ask him before letting him lead me toward his classroom.

We take several turns but after a couple minutes, we make it to his class. The room is brightly decorated and full of energetic kids who are dodging their fathers' attempts at getting them to calm down.

Huxley's teacher takes the attendance before we're all ushered from the room to go to the cafeteria where we will binge on donuts.

I have little interest in eating a donut since I already had a big breakfast this morning, but I help Huxley gather a couple of donuts and I take a coffee before finding us a seat at one of the tables.

Huxley has been chattier since we got to the cafeteria, so I'm hopeful he got over whatever nerves were getting him earlier. He's been pointing out classmates to me and telling me about his friends. He's almost done eating his first donut when a boy and his father take up seats opposite of us and Huxley noticeably tenses. He doesn't look at either of them, but it's clear he is aware of their presence.

"I thought you didn't have a dad," the boy says. At first, I didn't know who he was talking to but then I saw Huxley's head jerk up.

"That's not true." Comes his meek reply.

"What's this about Timmy?" The man with the boy asks.

He then goes on to talk about how Hux doesn't have a dad and makes some comments about believing he would be alone at the event. He almost sounds disappointed to see someone with Huxley, as if he would revel in his potential misery.

The man almost seems chagrin at his son's behavior but not in an authentic way. He reaches a hand across to me and introduces himself as Harrison DuPont.

"Rafael Quinn," I reply. I don't bother to fake niceties, my tone devoid of warmth.

His eyes bug out for a minute when the recognition takes place. He asks, "Rafael Quinn of the Triple Twisters?"

"Yes!" Huxley beams. "Raf owns the Triple Twisters." He gives me a proud look.

The boy loves baseball so much. It's something he enjoys playing but he also has been meeting a lot of the players and learning the secrets of the baseball world. There have been several times that he's hung out with our team while Jenny worked on some of the photography projects. Usually, he spent that time being regaled of tales from Jenson and Chad. They take great pleasure in telling tales of their monumental feats. Huxley revels in the attention and the history.

"Why do you call your dad Raf?" The boy sneered.

His father, Harrison, looked at Huxley curiously but didn't tell his son that it was an impolite question.

Hux tried a few times to explain, stumbling over his attempted words before finally saying, "Well, Raf is kind of my new Dad. My old Dad couldn't come today."

This little shit kid kept on asking all kinds of invasive questions and being snarky. He wanted to know why we had the same last name if he wasn't 'my son'.

His dad seemed to perk up, like a lightbulb going off, and said, "Wait a minute, I thought I heard something recently about you marrying your brother's wife."

I scowled at the man. I didn't marry his *wife*; I married his *ex*-wife. She was *my* wife now. Just like these kids would also be my kids. This all might have started as an agreement of mutual necessity but the whole family had grown on me. They were my family.

With a few clipped words, I shut down Harrison 'Butt-face' DuPont and Buttface Jr. The judgment from them was too harsh to be ignored and I knew that something would have to be done to rectify this situation. Huxley was a little boy; he didn't need to have people referring to him as the fatherless boy or sneering at the situation between his mother and me. I'd be having words about this in the future when Huxley wasn't around to see the verbal sparring.

Fourteen

Jenny

"Are you sure that you can handle this?" I ask Sara as I nervously fiddle with the handle of my suitcase in the entryway.

She smiled indulgently at me, as if to say, *quit being a chicken and get out of here.* "We'll be fine Jenny. Stop worrying. The kids will be fine without you for a couple of days. We got all the snacks they could want, and Rae put together a schedule of movies for us to stream. I 'haven't lived until I've seen these movies.'" She quoted what must have been Rae's words and I couldn't help but hear her voice say it in a sassy tone in my head.

With Sara's reassurances, I decided it was time to get over my nerves and finally leave. I knew the kids would be fine here with her, that wasn't my problem. What wrecked my nerves was the fact that while away for three nights I was going to be alone in a hotel room each night with my husband. The husband that I've been having filthy fantasies about for weeks, ever since our little incident in the bathroom. After he got me off with my vibrator, neither of us brought it up. It almost felt like something I dreamed but I knew it wasn't. The heat in his eyes was my daily reminder that it happened.

One flight, a couple of hours, and one cab ride later I arrived at the hotel. After checking in I headed to our room to drop off my suitcase.

The room was empty, but it was clear Rafael had been here recently. I could smell remnants of his cologne in the air. Unable to help it I sucked in a deep breath. Ugh, this man was turning me into a lustful freak who was desperate to even just smell him. What had my life turned into?

Irritated with myself I put my suitcase on the bed determined to get everything situated and get to work. I rummaged around until I found my camera bag. I checked my batteries and memory cards before changing out the lens. Strap placed around my neck and gear bagged I was ready to meet up with the team.

I'm here for business, I reminded myself as I headed downstairs.

The concierge helped me order a ride to take me to the stadium and it didn't take too long since it was still early before the game.

Tonight would be the first of three consecutive games that the Triple Twisters would play against their biggest rivals. The game would start at four, so I had a few hours to get to the stadium and do some behind the scenes type of photos of players beforehand. The fans have been loving the pre-game content that I've captured that the social media employees have been posting lately. They like seeing the players hanging out before the games, getting into a battle mindset, laughing with each other, etc.

Earlier when the plane landed and I turned off the airplane mode there was a text from Raf telling me where to go when I arrived, so I instructed the driver around the back to the entrance that was designated for employees and players.

The driver pulled up to the door and I knew with one hundred percent certainty I was in the right spot because a man was standing there holding a sign that said 'Mrs. Quinn' written in all caps.

I tipped the cabbie and got out, approaching the man slightly skeptically and asking, "Are you looking for Jenny Quinn?"

"Yes ma'am, I am!" He beamed at me but there was a gleam in his eyes that was unnerving.

It was a little strange but whatever, maybe Raf needed to talk to me before I got started. So, I followed the man as he led me inside.

Holding the door open for me he ushered me inside, where he tossed his sign into the trash can closest to the door.

We walked in an uncomfortable silence as he took me around multiple corners eventually leading towards a hallway that was fairly quiet and gave me a bit of the heebie-jeebies.

An internal alarm was sounding in my head, insisting that something about this situation wasn't quite right. I discreetly pulled my cell phone from the side pocket of my camera bag. I planned to shoot off a quick text to Raf but with a foreboding sense of dread, I saw the icon at the corner that indicated I didn't have service here.

My pulse hammered frantically in my neck even though nothing bad had happened yet. It just felt like something was going to happen.

I was about to stop and reconsider following this man when he stopped in front of a door.

"Here we are," he said in a jovial tone.

"We're where?" I asked him as I eyed him suspiciously.

"I was asked to bring you here to meet Mr. Quinn, of course." He kept his tone even, and he was trying hard to convey a look of total innocence. But I still didn't like this. It didn't feel right.

I patted my pockets before saying, "Oh shoot! It looks like I accidentally left my media pass in the cab that dropped me off. I better call them back right quick." Starting to back up I smiled at him, trying to look like I was just a ditzy idiot.

"We can get you a new pass." He stated firmly, taking a step toward me.

"Nonsense, that's too much trouble. It'll only take me a second, I'm sure the cabbie is still nearby waiting for his next fare. Thanks for showing me the way, I'll come back after I grab my pass." I said trying to convey that I was dismissing him while maintaining a friendly demeanor.

I was going to back up more but before I could he lunged at me and forced me through the door. When I passed the entryway, he shut the door from the outside and there was an audible click that sounded ominous in the quiet of the room.

Panicking I grabbed that handle and tried to turn it despite the soul-deep knowing that I was locked in. When I confirmed the door was locked from the outside I started banging on it. The man locked me in, so I was sure the chances were slim, but I still called out to him, pretending it was an accident, asking him to open the door. He didn't answer and no sound came from that side of the door. It was looking more and more like he left after trapping me here.

I gave up banging on the door when it became clear that no one would be coming to my rescue. For a minute I let fear grip me as I rested my head against the door. But I knew I couldn't stay in this mindset of defeat. I have two small kids who rely on me to love and care for them. I would not stay here wallowing in my crappy luck and give in to whatever bad thing was going to happen here.

After my mental pep talk, I straightened and prepared to survey my dark surroundings to get a better idea of where I was.

It was hard to get a good look at the room with the darkness. I slide my hands up the walls on both sides of the door searching for a light switch and coming up with none.

I started to move away from the door to get a better look at the room when I heard a noise from the other side. I squawked awkwardly from the fright. A door was opened, and a couple of thudding footsteps proceeded the sound of the door shutting once again.

"Ah, Mrs. Quinn so lovely to meet you." A deep voice said from the other side of the room before a bright light was flipped on momentarily blinding me.

Fifteen

Raf

"Start over, from the beginning," I demand as I resume pacing the length of the hotel room.

Jenny, who has told me the story multiple times, is holding her composure better than I am. It's hard to fathom how she's so calm when I'm ready to storm into that asshole's domain and break any part of his body I can get my hands on.

She repeats the same story once again. Telling me all the details from arriving at the stadium, and being ushered around by a man she never met under the guise of being led to me. She was shoved into a dark room that she was locked into and finally concluded with what happened with the owner of the team we were playing.

"Like I said," she pauses to swallow a drink of water, "once Mr. Carmichael showed up, he tried hitting on me. I told him off and I exited out of the door he had come in through."

Generally, I'm a levelheaded guy but this whole situation has me all riled up. First and foremost, I'm pissed off that Carmichael scared Jenny. I want nothing more than her safety and happiness, during our marriage, and beyond. Second, how fucking dare he. Where would that asshole get the idea, he could put a move on *my* woman, my *wife.*

This marriage might not be real in the normal sense but only we know that, to the world, it's as real as it gets.

I was so deep in my thoughts, imagining punching Carmichael in his smug face, that I didn't notice Jenny approaching me until she grabbed ahold of my lapels to stop my pacing.

"Raf, I'm okay. I promise." She tells me with a timid smile as she smooths her hand down my suit jacket.

I think she was going for a calming effect with the gesture, but it doesn't help. What it does help is making me extremely turned on.

It might have been an innocent touch, but I've been longing for her hands on my body. Craving her like a drug since the night I walked into the bathroom and caught her in the throes of pleasure. If I'm honest with myself my craving for her started long before that. I've wanted her since the day I saw her at my brother's house. She looked like a fierce goddess as she told him off and stood up to him. I had never seen something hotter.

My head jerks up and we lock eyes. I think she must be able to see what I've been denying myself because the next moment she stands on the tips of her toes, hands resting on my shoulders as she brings her mouth to mine.

Her lips are soft and warm as they pillow comfortingly around mine. The kiss is a tentative thing, a barely there caress. In my current state, it breaks the chains on all I've been withholding from her. My restraint snaps and I kiss her back with more fervor.

My deepening of the kiss seemed to momentarily stun her, almost as if she thought I would reject her. Once she realizes that I'm not only accepting her affections but amplifying it back she doesn't hold back.

Her arms wrap around my neck, bringing her chest against mine. My arms instinctually go under her ass, lifting her, bringing her closer to me. Her legs wrap around me as I carry her to the bed.

It's like coordinated chaos as we both shred off our clothes. My suit jacket hits the floor without a care. Her shirt gets flung across the room landing on a lamp.

Our kisses are frantic as she pulls me down onto the bed, causing me to land on top of her.

My hand comes up and I slowly slide it across her clit. Keeping my touch feather-light. She grabs my wrist forcefully and inserts two of my fingers inside of her. The move took me off guard but was so fucking hot.

My sexy-as-hell wife didn't enjoy my teasing touch and demanded what she wanted. Good. She could have me any way she wants me. I will give her anything and everything she demands of me. I've been a goner for her from the very beginning.

My cock throbs almost painfully at the idea of being inside her but I take my time playing with her pussy. I want her not just wet but dripping for me.

My thumb rubs circles on her clit while my fingers continue a tantalizing rhythm, pumping in and out of her. I work them in a scissoring motion, helping stretch her a bit in preparation for my dick.

By the time my hand is soaked, her moans are like a symphony in our room. The sweetest sounds I've ever heard. I want it to be the soundtrack to my life forever more.

"Raf, please."

"Please what *wife*?" I tease.

"Please, I need you. I've been needing you." She pants as she tries to wiggle more intensely against my hand.

"What do you need from me?" I ask refusing to give in so easily.

Her voice comes out even more frustrated as she finally says, "I need your cock. I need you to fuck me. Please."

With her words whip-sharp in the air between us, I remove my hand from her. With my tip lined up at her entrance, I claim her lips once more before thrusting fully into her causing us both to moan.

Grabbing both her knees I lift her into a position where I can access deep into her core.

We both moan as her walls squeeze me tight. I rock back and forth, pulling almost out of her before sliding back in. The slick smooth glide is a beautiful thing. My fingers work her clit as we continue to gyrate together.

We both become a sweaty mess as we rock together bringing each other to pleasure. As soon as her orgasm hits my release finds me as well.

For several long minutes, we lay entangled breathing hard in the aftermath of what is now the second-best moment of my life—the first being the day I married her.

Sixteen

Jenny

After the initial night of our away trip, we spent the remaining days sequestered in our hotel room. Raf was worked up and refused to allow me to return to the stadium afterward. He didn't go back either, instead opting to stay with me. We spent those days tangled together in our newfound passion rather than returning home early.

I traveled back on the team plane instead of flying separately for the return flight. It was an exciting atmosphere due to the celebrations taking place from the players. The Triple Twisters won all three of the games against their biggest rivals, it was truly something to celebrate.

Both Chad and Jensen were hovering around Raf and me as they regaled us with the tales from the two games we had missed. They've become frequent guests at our house since Raf and I married, and I have grown to enjoy their company. They have been nothing but friendly and kind to my kids and myself.

Chad went into great detail about a series of strikes Jenson was able to throw against the competitors. "He had them out there looking like a little league team trying to bat against the big boys!"

"Nah," Jenson refuted, "I've seen Huxley's little league team and they hit better than them."

Jenson as well as a few others have attended a few of the games for Huxley's team since Raf has been attending. Many kids have been over the moon being in the presence of professional ball players. They have all been great with the kids and families. Fame hasn't changed these guys; they are still super down-to-earth and willing to be 'regular guys'. They have been encouraging the kids and helping give tips on ways for them to improve their gameplay.

Huxley has been enjoying all the extra attention from his teammates. They look at him like he's their hero because of the entourage of Triple Twister players he has been surrounding himself with. The gained comradery has boosted my sweet boy's confidence.

With all the conversation the flight passes quickly and before I know it, we are walking up to the house. Before we make it to the front door it swings open with a brutal speed.

Huxley squeals with excitement as he wraps his small arms around me, holding me tight before he rushes to Raf and repeats the action.

Rae emerges from the entryway at a much more sedate pace before greeting us both. Her reactions to Raf and his presence have grown warmer over these few months. At first, she was very hesitant to be around him or get to know him at all—which I find understandable. She's been let down by her father, the man who should do everything he can to protect and love her. She is hurting from the past and is skeptical of letting someone else into her life. There is a vulnerability that comes with bonding with someone new, you open yourself up to the possibility of getting hurt by them.

After all our greetings are exchanged, we enter the house and I look for Sarah. I find her in the kitchen pulling a dessert out of the oven.

"Oh good, you're back!" She exclaims.

"What's this?" I ask her, gesturing to the pie that smells of blueberries.

"Oh, Jack stopped by earlier. He said there would be a family dinner tonight at his house and he wanted to make sure I knew I was invited. I figured if you were okay with me going, I would make a little treat to bring so I didn't come empty-handed."

"Yes, we have dinner there tonight and of course you can come. We would be happy to have you there." I glance again at the tempting dessert before asking the question that's been swirling in my mind for the past three days, "How did it go?"

She leaned back against a section of marble countertops, crossing her arms as she went. After releasing a breath she responds, "For the most part it was fine."

"Mostly fine." I reaffirm. When she nods her agreement, I press for more. "What were the not fine parts?"

"Well," she starts, "Rae had a little trouble one of the nights."

Guilt flooded me hearing that my baby girl was strug-gling while I was having fun and enjoying spending time with my temporary husband.

"She was crying loud enough that I heard her, and she ended up waking up while I was on my way to see what was wrong."

"Did she have a nightmare?"

"She said she missed her dad and was asking to see him. I told her that he was sleeping because it was the middle of the night and then snuggled with her for a little bit until she settled down. I know things are precarious with him and he doesn't often keep his word, so I didn't want to offer her false promises, but I figured you'd want to know."

I thanked her before leaving the room. I had to get away for a minute alone. My eyes were filling with angry tears as I walked away. It gutted me that Carlos could be so distant from the kids. He didn't ever ask to see them, couldn't hold up his end of our arrangements when he was scheduled visits, wouldn't help with any of their expenses, or show up to their events. It hurt to know he cared so little for the lives he helped create. He should be nurturing them, loving them, and supporting them. He had shown his true colors and unfortunately, our kids were caught in the middle of this mess.

Seventeen

Raf

Wildness came with us as we entered my dad's house. Before Jenny and her kids came into my life I was used to my quiet life. After meeting Jenny there were very few minutes not surrounded by noise and movement. I thought it would take more getting used to, but somehow it didn't take long for me to adjust. Now I felt like I thrived on the chaos.

Once I got used to someone always being around it made me realize how lonely my life had been. In the months since Jenny and the kids moved into my house, we've all grown close. I'm used to Jenny being my sounding board and closest friend. I'm used to Huxley's sports trivia and big imagination. I'm used to coaxing Rae out of the castle of imaginary bricks she's built to protect herself, getting her to slowly lower the walls.

I've come to release that I love them, all of them. I never knew something was missing from my life but it's so clear now.

With only a few months left to this agreement between Jenny and me, I need to figure out how to keep her—because I am going to keep her.

"My favorite people!" Da yells when we walk into his home.

The kids both run straight to him and hug him around his legs as Jenny reminds them to take it easy on him.

Sara gives a coy smile to my father. His responding grin feels time-stopping. He's been muddling through life since my mother died but lately, he seems almost like his old self. I only wish he could have more time. More happiness before we all have to say our goodbyes.

Dad and I catch up about the away trip while setting the table. We go over player stats and discuss the upcoming game schedules with Huxley hanging on to our every word. I can invision a future like this for us, with him grown and bringing his own kids to see Jenny and me, talking through strategy for running our baseball empire.

Jenny and Sara bring all the food to the table so we can eat. Dad's cook prepared arroz con pollo. Its ease of preparation and its stomach-filling abilities made it one of my mother's favorite family dinners when I was growing up. She used to make it so much that for a while in my teen years I got sick of eating it. Of course once my mother passed away it was a comfort food when I missed her.

The large dish full of the meal gets passed around the table and I help put some on Huxley's plate. He observes it with a look of suspicion as he pokes at it with his fork.

"Do I have to eat these vegetables?" He asks me from the corner of his mouth. He's trying to keep quiet so his mom doesn't overhear, no doubt she would say yes, he needs to eat them.

I whisper back to him like we are sharing a secret, "I won't tell if you won't."

He laughs a little before scooping up a bite of the chicken.

We eat our dinner with a continuous stream of chatter and just as we are handing out slices of Sara's blueberry pie the front door opens with a *bang*.

"Are you expecting any guests?" I ask Dad.

From the look of confusion on his face, I infer the answer is a resounding no.

I'm about to push out of my seat to investigate when my brother Carlos bursts into the room.

The way he's swaying and stumbling divulges the fact that he is intoxicated.

"Daddy!" Rae yells excitedly.

She runs toward him arms out, wanting to hug him but he walks right past her without acknowledgment.

He storms to the table and almost topples over when he gets closer. Arm out he starts sweeping items off the table, making them clatter to the floor, breaking things.

Rae's bottom lip quivers at the rejection from her father. Huxley gives me a questioning look. Both kids look scared and his behavior is unacceptable.

Standing from my seat to intervene I'm beaten to it by Jenny who's closer.

"What the heck is wrong with you?" She demands.

He points a finger back and forth between her and me before brusquely asking, "What the hell is this? I guess it's true."

"What's true?" She asks him.

He gets this look on his face and from growing up with him I know whatever is about to come from his mouth can't be anything good.

"This!" He points at us again. He stomps his foot like a petulant child before stating, "That you're whoring yourself out to my brother!"

Sara who had the forethought to drag the kids out of the room when he started the impromptu table clearing comes back into the room to check on my father.

Jenny tries to respond to him but all I see is red. Who is he to make these types of accusations, especially with what he put Jenny through during their marriage?

No one talks to my wife like that. Especially not him.

Before I even realize what I'm doing I'm in his face. My fist connects fiercely with his jaw.

He tumbles to the floor with a shocking ease. He looks up at me like he doesn't recognize me. But if I'm being honest, I'm not sure I would even recognize myself. I'm not usually the violent type, but Jenny deserves better. She isn't going to be put through this.

"Get up," I demand as my hands go under his arms.

I haul his body from the floor with very little help from him.

We emerge from the entryway and opening the door I toss him out of the house.

"Rafael, what the fuck?" He spits with disgust.

"You don't get to talk to her like that. In fact, you don't get to talk to her at all."

I pull my phone out of my pocket and order him a ride. The I plant myself in front of the door, guarding it until a car pulls up to pick him up.

When the driver comes to a stop, I point to it and tell him, "You've more than overstayed your welcome."

Once gets into the car I head back inside and try to clean up the mess he made, both the physical and emotional mess.

Eighteen

Raf

Ever since the night of the interrupted dinner at Dad's house, Rae has been even more melancholy. It's hard to see someone so young and sweet go through so much. She deserves to be treated with all the love and kindness in the world. She started to close herself off from everyone, which was hard to witness, so I decided to try to do something about it.

After a week of her glum mood, I struck up a conversation about a book she was reading. It turns out the book was part of a series, and I talked my way into us starting an unofficial book club.

Over the past month, we've read one book from the series each week. Each week the unicorn girls from the book series go on a different adventure. This week they meet and join a group of Valkyries.

The book series being for young readers is easy to read and I can honestly say I didn't think I would enjoy it as much as I have. The writer makes them both informative but also humorous.

So here we are for another book club 'meeting', sitting on the child-size beanbags surrounded by her jungle of plants.

My legs are squashed up to my chest as I flip through my copy of the book. I think if we keep up reading together, we might need to relocate to the game room, so I have more legroom. Maybe once she's more comfortable I can talk to her about it. At first, I wanted to make this as easy as possible for her to agree to, I wanted her to be comfortable enough to participate.

Rae's favorite character is Storme who happens to be the fiercest of the unicorn girls. She's always the first one to jump into trying new things and the most loyal protector of her band of friends. It's clear from what she says about Storme that Rae looks up to her character tremendously.

As we are discussing the historical details related to Valkyries, their myths, and legends I see a shadow pass by the open doorway.

I covertly peek to see who walked by, but the person didn't walk by, Jenny stands just out of sight of Rae looking in on us.

She gives me a smile that is as sad as it is happy.

When Rae and I are done discussing the book I tell her she can pick the next book. She decided upon one where the unicorn girls become fighter pilots.

After she is all tucked into bed, I close the door and head to the main bedroom.

Entering the room, I see Jenny tucked under the blankets while propped up against the headboard.

"Hey," she whispers when she sees me.

I lean over her and plant a sweet kiss on her lips. "Hey," I reply.

"How did it go?" She asks me.

"Oh, we had lots of fun. This week was about Valkyries, you'll have to watch out, I think she's going to ask you about warrior training before long." I tell her with a chuckle.

She gives an exasperated sigh before feigning irritation as she says, "Great."

Straightening up and looking more seriously at me she asks, "You know you don't have to do this right?"

"Of course. However, I enjoy the time with Rae, and it seems to be helping us bond. And while it might sound weird, those books are funny. I've been finding the experience enjoyable."

Still within her reach she grabs me and hauls me down into the bed. Stradling my body she leans down, kissing me before she rewards me for my efforts late into the night.

Nineteen

Jenny

I was about to sit down at the dinner table when Rafael arrived home for the evening.

He had a meeting that would run long. Since I made it home from work earlier tonight than he did I volunteered to make the meal. The kids begged for a breakfast dinner tonight, so I made delicious French toast with maple sausage links.

He enters the dining room with a dark wooden box held between his hands. I'm not sure what is in it, but he looks very satisfied about something.

He gives Rae a quick hug as he passes before stopping in front of Huxley and ruffling his unruly hair.

Huxley squeals in delight and tries to escape the attack on his head. Raf teases him before straightening back to his full height.

"I got something I think you'll like." He says before holding the box toward Hux.

"Me?" Huxley points to his chest in confusion.

"Yeah, bud." Handing it to Huxley he gestures to it and says, "Go ahead and open it up."

We watch on as Huxley pulls a ribbon from around it. I glance at Rafael curious as to what will be inside and chuckle when I see him rubbing his hands together with excitement. Sometimes he reminds me of an overgrown kid—with his sense of enjoyment—and it is one of his many endearing qualities.

The ribbon hits the floor as it's unceremoniously flung away from the box.

When the lid is lifted an unearthly screech leaves Huxley's mouth before he starts tearing around the room like a tornado.

Rae huffs, annoyed about the anticlimactic unveiling, seeing as we are all left in suspense about the mystery contents.

"Well, what is it?" She demands.

Huxley finally seems to calm down enough to reveal stacks of baseball cards. His baseball card collection is his most prized possession, but this greatly surpasses the cards he owns. In the box are signed cards.

"I worked a little magic and was able to get autographed card copies of all the Triple Twister players," Rafael states in a matter-of-fact tone as if what he did was no big deal. But to my sweet little boy, this was probably the biggest deal.

Hux threw himself at Rafael, who promptly brought himself down to his level for the hug.

Tears caught in the corner of my eye as I watched them.

Somehow this man who entered a bargain with me, a stranger, has become an integral part of this little family of mine. It was sweet to witness the growing bond between him and my kids but bitter for the fact that this was all temporary.

Now isn't the time to worry about it I chided internally. We most likely still have a few months before we meet the end of our countdown clock.

Just as I talked myself down from the mental cliff of despair a ringing started. I looked at my phone after pulling it out of my pocket only to see it wasn't my phone that was ringing.

Standing up Rafael pulled his phone out and answered it.

"No," he said, in such a guttural tone.

Everything seemed to stop as I held my breath waiting to see what was wrong. But the sinking feeling in my gut told me what I already knew.

He whispered into the phone from the edge of the room before thanking the person on the other line and hanging up.

When he turned to me the look of pure anguish, he wore was like a baseball bat to the gut.

"Jack?" I asked him. I didn't need to elaborate for him to understand.

He nodded the tiniest bit before whispering, "He's gone."

And so, starts the beginning of the end.

Twenty

Raf

No matter how hard I try it's near impossible to wrap my mind around the fact that one week ago my father died. I've known for a while this day would eventually get here but I thought we had more time—as cliché as that is.

I've barely muddled through the days since he passed. If not for Jenny, I don't think I'd be anywhere near functional. That saint of a woman has been my rock, helping significantly with the preparations and arrangements for the funeral.

It's not often that I use a driver unless it's for work trips but today it felt necessary to rely on Jasper to get our family to the service safely.

He navigates the crowd that's started to gather at the funeral home and pulls to a stop in front of the entrance. With a nod of thanks in his direction, I exit the car before leaning back toward the door and extending my hand back in to help Jenny out.

Rae and Huxley follow behind her, our group is accompanied by Sara who we insisted ride with us. She has been spending a lot of time at our house helping with the kids. We recently transitioned to her being a hired caregiver for the kids when we have work or other events we need to attend. Though the type of person Sara is, she would be here regardless of being an employee. She loves Rae and Huxley, treating them as if they are her grandkids. Sometimes I think if my dad hadn't been sick, they would have made a good couple; they got along well and seemed to enjoy each other's company.

Even though we were dropped in front of the main door it takes several minutes for us to get inside since people keep stopping us to pay their respects. It's bittersweet seeing the turnout, knowing that my father was loved by so many people from all walks of life, and knowing the impact he must have made on their lives.

We take the seats at the front that are reserved for the family. In what feels like seconds, but is much longer, the funeral is over. My worthless brother didn't even bother to show—can't say I'm that shocked about it, but I hoped for better from him. Guess I'm just another person he's disappointed.

Once back to the car, Jasper follows behind the hearse, leading the procession to the cemetery that contains my father's burial plot, which lies next to my mother's resting place.

We surround the minister as he gives final words before we lay him to rest. Before leaving the cemetery, I make sure to stop at my mother's grave and leave her some flowers. I try to imagine them being reunited if only to soothe some of my melancholy.

We dropped Sara and the kids off back at home before Jenny and I proceeded to my father's house for the wake that was planned. Only our extended family members on my father's side and close friends would be in attendance but since drinking and possible rowdiness might occur, we figured it was best for the children to not be in attendance.

We arrived at Dad's house and upon entry I noted that one of his staff members must have helped with preparations. The windows were open slightly and the mirrors were covered.

Jenny crossed over to the bar in the living area and poured a drink before bringing it to me. Once it was in my hand, she wrapped her arms around my waist. Her silent support gave me the level of comfort I was grateful for.

When the house was packed full of bodies of loved ones, everyone started sharing fond memories and stories of my father's life.

Twenty-One

Raf

Pulling open the glass door I enter the office of the prestigious law firm my father has trusted for decades to handle of his legal affairs. Since we used the same firm for our team contracts, I was familiar with the staff and was able to greet the receptionist by name when I checked in for our meeting.

With my dad's death being inevitable he was well prepared with a will, so things were left as mess-free as possible. It's been two weeks since the funeral, and the only delay to the will reading was waiting for the lawyer to have an opening, he has been kept busy with a trial that has thankfully just ended.

The receptionist, Margie, leads me to a conference room on the other side of the state-of-the-art building. When we enter the room there are several lawyers seated at the large wooden table, as well as my brother.

It's irritating to me that he couldn't be bothered to come to Dad's funeral or help with any of the arrangements leading up to it but not only was he more than willing to attend this meeting and showed up early. I guess the motivation was there since I'm sure he expects to gain something from Dad's estate.

"Thanks for coming in," Mr. Locklair my father's lawyer said to me as he gave me a firm handshake in greeting.

"Thank you for fitting us into your schedule as soon as you could. I know you've been keeping busy lately," I returned.

Pulling out the remaining empty chair I sat down to join the others. The chair was surprisingly comfortable to sit in, maybe I should check the brand and try to get a similar one for my office.

My brother had a slimy look about him when he met my eyes across the table. The time since I punched his face has been sufficient that there was no bruise evident today, pity. I hoped he would bear the mark of my fury a little longer. I'm not normally someone prone to violence of any sort but I felt unhinged hearing the words he spoke to Jenny, my sweet Jenny didn't deserve to carry the hurt of his words. It was also deserved for his treatment of Rae and Huxley, the way he completely ignored them to pitch his fit.

Carlos looked smug as he greeted me, "Ah, brother. So good to see you again." He smirked before making a generalized statement about how we would be seeing a lot more of each other very soon, the implication was clear, he believed he would receive Dad's shares of the baseball team and we would be stuck working together regularly.

If Dad wasn't convinced about Carlos' lack of moral character that notion had been corrected at the dinner he interrupted. Dad was severely upset by the incident and when the kids weren't around Jenny explained in depth some of the details, he didn't know the toxicity involved with her marriage to Carlos, including the reasons for the divorce. It deeply hurt our father to know that his son had taken such a negative turn in life.

So, he could sit there and look smug, but the joke would be on him if he was expecting those shares, I knew he wouldn't be getting them.

The receptionist offered everyone freshly brewed coffee and some refreshments before leaving so the meeting could commence.

One of the lawyers whose name I was unsure of opened a dark brown leather briefcase and pulled out some printed documents before passing them to Mr. Locklair.

"Thank you, Jonathon," he said to the lawyer as he took the stack of papers.

After he was finished getting situated, he started the long process of listing out all my father's possessions and their intended distribution.

An hour and a half later we were finished with the reading, and I was on my way out of the building. I walked out alone as my brother had left part way through when he found out he wouldn't be receiving the shares of the Triple Twisters that he thought he would own.

What was left to Carlos amounted to approximately fifty thousand dollars of value, none of which was cash. I think what he received reflected my father's disappointment in him.

The gist of the will's important parts was that my father's shares of our team were split up amongst Rae, Huxley, and me; the house was left to me. He made me the executor over the shares he gave the kids until they turn 21 at which point, they will gain access to them. He also left each of them a large trust that they could start drawing funds from upon turning eighteen, lump sums available periodically, ending at twenty-five.

It's a relief that Carlos will not be a part of managing the Triple Twisters. The shares being split between Rae and Huxley was a great choice considering he wanted the kids to be involved in it in the future if they so desired.

Twenty-Two

Jenny

A wave of emotion threatened to drown me as I looked at the papers sitting in front of me. I've been sitting here at the dining room table for thirty solid minutes just willing myself to get it over with.

With a deep breath, I fortify myself with invisible armor and reach forward for the pen. I unceremoniously remove the cap and in black ink sign my name.

A tear trickles down my cheek as I set the papers down in a stack and scrawl a short note for Rafael.

Today, one week from the will reading, everything is transferring to Raf. We've now accomplished everything we agreed to. I helped him keep Carlos at bay and he helped me get back on my feet.

When the will reading came through, I waited for him to say something about our arrangement. Waiting for him to give me the news about our ending. Waiting for him to say 'nice knowing you please leave'. He hasn't. But he also hasn't said anything about wanting to keep what we've found.

I can't keep waiting, it hurts too much. So, I made the decision easier. I had today off so I met with a lawyer who helped me draft a divorce petition, it was very straightforward since it will be uncontested, and we don't have any joint-owned property to split.

Walking away from the signed papers, I feel like I'm leaving a part of my heart behind, and it's not far from the truth because I fell for Raf. I don't know when it happened, but somewhere along the way it did.

Walking up the stairs I head to the kids' bedrooms to start packing up the essentials. I've scheduled for a moving company to come this weekend and get the rest.

In Huxley's room, I grab a few changes of clothes for him as well as his favorite stuffy to sleep with, and most importantly his baseball card collection.

When I go into Rae's room, I start much the same but as I'm bagging up the clothes my eyes drift to the two child-sized bean bag chairs. Closing my eyes briefly I can picture the night when I saw Raf and her sitting there talking about the unicorn books they had been reading together. My baby girl's laughter as they discussed the unlikelihood of unicorns training as Valkyries and holding swords. A small smile tips my lips at the corner just for a second as I savor the memory.

It breaks my heart to think about how our leaving might affect my babies. But this was never supposed to be permanent, I knew that going in. I didn't know they would grow so close with Raf, and I can only hope their hearts will mend from the disappointment they will surely feel.

The current unicorn book they are working on, one where the unicorns learn about Rosie the Riveter and how women impacted the efforts during World War II, sits atop one of the bean bags. I'm unsure if Rae will want to finish it without Rafael or not but just in case, I grab her copy and put it in the bag.

When I'm in our bedroom I grab my stuff but without much thought, I snag a soft hoodie that Rafael wore last night. It still smells like him. The hoodie is added to my bag. Maybe it will be of some comfort to me when I struggle with missing him.

With one last glance around the room, I shut the door behind me.

When I picked the kids up from school, I tried to keep a reassuring smile on my face. I was trying to hold myself together as I started driving. The ruse didn't last long, approximately ten minutes into the drive Rae my ever-observant child pointed out that we were going the wrong way.

"Where are we going?" She asked.

"We're going home." I smiled, trying to not make a big deal about it.

"No this is the opposite way of home," Rae grumbled from the back.

"We are going to *our* home," I replied.

"What do you mean?" Huxley asked concerned.

"We will be going back home. I packed some stuff to get us through the rest of the week, this weekend movers will bring us the rest of our stuff."

Both kids started panicking. They were confused about why we weren't going home to Raf and honestly, it was hard for me to explain, especially when my emotions were still so raw.

When we pulled up to the old place Rae flung her door open as soon as we entered the driveway, before I had even put the car in park, and ran full steam toward the front door. She didn't wait for me to get to the porch before she unlocked the door using her key and slammed the door.

Huxley wouldn't look at me as we unpacked our bags.

It hurt to know that I caused harm to my babies by going along with this bargain with Raf. We were at a point where we didn't have a lot of options because it was such a struggle doing it all on my own, when the opportunity arose, I didn't have much choice but to accept because of how dire everything was. But still, I felt horrible to know they were hurting, and it was a direct result of something I did.

Twenty-Three

Raf

What. A. Day. I thought as I leaned, resting against the backseat of the car.

Jasper drove me today so I could answer emails and such for work since I was out of the office for most of the day.

Everything was signed to officially gain everything that my dad's will left to me. Carlos had to show up too so he could sign for his stuff as well. He was still trying to act petty about the team, but the lawyer verified that there was no means of recourse for him to appeal the verdict.

It gave me great satisfaction to see him try to argue with the lawyer only to fail. I can't wait to tell Jenny about it.

Jasper pulls up out front of my house and right away I notice something strange. Jenny's car is usually in the driveway by now but right now it isn't there.

She didn't have work today but even if she did, she would normally be home by now. The kids got out of school over an hour ago and I know she had planned to pick them up herself today instead of Sara getting them.

I check my phone to see if I missed any calls or texts. Nothing. If there was an emergency surely, she would have called me, that thought is slightly reassuring. No one is dead or hurt at least.

After I thank Jasper, I walk briskly to the door and when I walk inside all that meets me is silence. The lights aren't even turned on.

I flip the switch so I can look around and nothing looks out of place at first. I go upstairs and start noticing little things here and there that are missing.

Not finding anyone home I decide to go back downstairs. I pull my phone back out and call Jenny while I get water from the fridge.

Her phone rings. And rings. And rings. Eventually, it goes to voicemail.

There's this unnamable nervous feeling sitting like a rock in my stomach and I can't put a finger on why.

Grabbing a glass from the cupboard to pour my water into, I turn toward the table. Sitting on the table is a stack of papers with a folded note on top. Seeing my name written on the outside I pick it up.

Inside it reads:

Raf,

Thank you for everything. I wanted to make this easier for us both. My section is signed. If you could sign these and send them in, we can finalize our arrangement.

—J

Finalize what? I wonder as I pick up the paperwork. My stomach bottoms out when I see *'petition for divorce'* at the top with Jenny and my name listed.

No. Not happening. I will not let this happen.

Our relationship hasn't been about an agreement in months. It became so much more than that. Being with Jenny felt like being complete. She became so much more than I ever imagined. She felt like finding home and once you've experienced that, you'd be an idiot to let it pass you by.

I thought we were on the same page but now I realize that I should have been more explicit in my intentions. We should have talked about this. I should have asked her to stay.

Now that I know why Jenny isn't here, I've got work to do. She would've gone back to the house she lived in before moving in with me. My lip curled into a sneer just thinking about that rundown place. She and the kids deserve so much better than that and I was going to make sure they got it.

Grabbing my keys, I sprinted to my car and headed to fight for my wife. My kids. My family.

Twenty-Four

Jenny

Wearing Rafael's stolen hoodie, I lay curled up on my old lumpy couch.

When I got home the kids essentially gave me the cold shoulder and shut themselves away in their room. I've tried checking on them, but they were not too happy about it.

My heart hurts tonight and I'm sure it'll hurt for a while. I just hope the kids will let me be there for them soon, so they are not processing the changes alone.

Tonight, I will lay here a while and feel my emotions, tomorrow I will pull myself together, for myself but mostly for my kids.

Reaching for the bottle of wine on the coffee table I take another gulp of the sweet Moscato. It was a lucky find when I went searching to see if anything was remaining in the kitchen.

I lay back on the couch but before my head hits the armrest there is a sharp squeal of tires outside. *Shit.* It sounded like it was right outside our place. Huffing I get up to check it out.

I toss off the throw blanket I was snuggling with and start walking toward the door just as a loud pounding starts.

Hopefully, the noise doesn't wake the kids up since last I checked they were sleeping.

Hurrying to open the door I do something outside of the norm, I don't look to see who it is.

Pulling the door open sharply I'm shocked at the sight of a disheveled Carlos standing directly in front of me.

"You!" He yells before charging toward me with a look of malice written on his features.

Instinctually I step back, but before I can close the door in his face, he forces his way inside the house.

Grabbing my upper arm, he yanks me sideways, causing me to fall.

"This is all your fault," he accuses.

The unanticipated attack left me unprepared to sturdy myself and I cried out as I hit the ground.

I try to scoot further away from him as I ask, "What's my fault?"

His features seem too dark with my question.

My scurrying doesn't get me far since he steps toward me.

"You're the reason I lost everything!"

Lost everything? What was left for him to lose? He lost his wife and kids all on his own. He lost his father due to illness. There was nothing for me to take.

I try to respond, to try to find a way to placate him and de-escalate the situation. Before I can utter another word, he sits on my chest and then his hands are wrapped around my throat.

It's too hard to breathe, unable to get any air my lungs start to burn.

My mind starts to feel fuzzy.

I think he's going to kill me. I'm going to die with so many things unfinished and dreams unfulfilled.

As my ears are pounding the slow sound of my heartbeat, everything starts to fade to black.

Beep. Beep. Beep.

An annoying noise starts to stir me from sleep.

Shifting in bed I try to get more comfortable but when I attempt to roll I'm stopped by something wrapped around my left arm.

With squinted eyes, I look around. The sight I'm greeted with is unexpected. I'm surrounded by walls a stark white and there are uncomfortably bright florescent lights above me.

At first, I was very confused, but then it started coming back to me. Leaving Raf's house, being home, opening the door, Carlos—he attacked me.

Tears accumulated behind my shut eyelids as I remembered what happened.

The beeping speeds up, getting more frequent.

"Jenny?" A gruff voice asks. It sounds like Rafael but different, raw.

Opening my eyes, I turn my head in the direction the voice came from. Standing in the doorway is Rafael, looking the worst I've ever seen him. He looks tormented.

There is no holding back the tears now. What's he doing here? Did the hospital call him since we aren't divorced yet?

"Raf?" My voice came out a barely heard whisper despite speaking at full volume. The attempt to speak hurts.

Throbbing pain erupts in my throat causing a whimper to slip out.

Rafael crosses the room quickly, wrapping me in his arms. "Shh," he soothes.

The crying only gets worse as I bury my face in his chest.

He just hugs me tighter, holding me through it.

When my breathing eases and I've got better control of myself I peek up at Rafael.

"What are you doing here?" I rasp.

"I'm so glad you're okay," he states before clearing his throat. He looks like he is suffering hard emotions as well. "If I was just a minute or two later, I don't think I would've made it in time."

Confused by his emotional declaration he continues to tell me about the events from his perspective. He found the note I left and was on his way to get me back. He had this grand speech planned and was going to rip up the divorce petition in front of me so I would know he was serious. He said he drove to my house, breaking speeding laws all along the way. He tells me about getting to my house and seeing the front door open. About walking in and seeing Carlos with his hands wrapped around my throat, my face blue from lack of air. About fighting Carlos off me and getting the police there. About me being brought to the hospital. Rafael saved my life.

When he is done telling me everything that happened, he looks me in the eyes, but his gaze feels like it penetrates my soul when he speaks.

"I'm sorry if I wasn't clear Jenny. I'm sorry if I didn't communicate my intentions effectively. But I'm so in love with you. When I came home to find your note, I knew I had to go after you. Please stay with me. Be my wife, for real."

My heart swells with emotions. With a small smile, I reply, "I love you too Rafael Quinn and nothing would make me happier than staying married to you."

After I'm released from the hospital we start the drive back to Rafael's home—*our* home. With everything that happened Sara is keeping the kids overnight at her house and will bring them home late tomorrow morning so it will be just us at the house.

I enter the house first and after Raf enters he turns around and shuts the door.

He slowly turns back to me and he stares at me with an intense look that is hard to read.

Stalking towards me slowly he looks like a predator on the hunt for prey.

"How are you feeling?" He asks me as he observes me, head tilted slightly.

"I feel fine. My throat hurts a bit but other than that I'm good." I reply to him.

A look of approval crosses his face, and finding my answer satisfactory he continues toward me.

"Good," he drawls. "We have some unfinished business." The latter he says in a deep whisper against my ear.

"What kind of business?" I question as a shiver causes bumps to coat my skin.

He draws back slightly and pulls out a piece of folded-up paper from his pants pocket. Once it's open he holds it aloft, displaying the signature page of the divorce document.

Eyes locked with mine he says, "The kind where you tried to leave me." He rips the paper down the middle before continuing, "I'm glad you changed your mind because I wouldn't have let you."

From another man that statement would have felt like a threat, but from Rafael, it makes my clit throb at the possessiveness he showed.

Picking me up he tosses me over his shoulder like a caveman as he starts stomping up the stairs. I try protesting being carried because let's face it I was never a tiny woman, but after two kids I kept a few extra pounds each time; he just gives me ass a playful smack and reminds me he was a professional athlete and that he loves my body. The latter he demonstrates by placing my hand on his erect cock which is straining against his slacks.

It takes no time at all for him to march us into our bedroom and kick the door shut behind them before he drops me to the bed.

The stern brunch daddy vibes he's giving off right now are working for me. Feeling needy I don't bother to wait for him to strip me, I start doing it myself.

He watches me hungrily as I remove the sweats I left the hospital in. Cursing mentally I wish I could have been wearing something sexier for our 'reunion' but Sara was kind enough to bring me some fresh clothes and this is what she found. Despite the wardrobe, the hungry way he looks at me makes me forget my worries.

We both divest ourselves of clothes with haste and then he climbs onto the bed with me.

His tongue slowly twines with mine in a seductive dance as he kisses me. His hand which started on my knee slides up the inside of my leg until he eventually makes it to my entrance.

Feeling that I'm already wet he doesn't spend long playing with me before rubbing his cock against my folds, coating himself with my slick desire.

When he has his tip against my center, he holds completely still, as he watches me he asks, "Are you ready to apologize?"

I nod frantically. "Yes." I pant. "I'm sorry. So sorry Raf."

As soon as the words leave my lips he thrusts into me and we spend that whole night making up and making love.

Epilogue

Raf

Fifteen Years Later

"Come on Dad," Mariella yells excitedly as she drags me through the crowd.

At fourteen she's come into her personality. She is the perfect mix of Jenny and me. She's already taller than Jenny and has her wavy hair but it's colored like mine. Her eyes are the same honey brown as Jenny's. She's sweet like her mom and a bit bossy like me, as evidenced by her behavior today.

We push into the glass room reserved for our family and stop to see Jenny and Rae before taking our seats.

Rae smiles excitedly when she sees us and exchanges a hug with Mariella. We saw each other earlier today at work as we have every day since she started training for her newly acquired position of team manager for the Triple Twisters. A position she worked hard to earn following her college graduation this past summer.

Jenny greets me with an attempted quick kiss which I greedily lengthen before the kids start hollering at us to 'knock it off' and 'stop being gross'.

"How is he looking?" I ask Rae as we survey the field below, looking for Huxley.

"He's nervous but he's doing a really good job keeping his cool. He looked great during warmups. His practice pitches were averaging 93 mph." She states while reviewing data on the tablet she is holding.

"Nice." I nod along as she tells me about his batting average.

Today's a big day and we were all excited to be here for it. Huxley will be pitching his first baseball game since signing in the majors.

We knew early on that he had ambitions of playing professional baseball. We were supportive of his choices; our only caveat was that we asked that he attend college and try college ball before ditching it. Which he did. He attended a year of college where he played college baseball but when inquiries from major scouts kept coming in, he talked to us about dropping his college courses and accepting an offer.

By the end of his first season of college ball, he had contract offers from five different teams, making him one of the most sought-after pitchers in recent years.

Of course, there was only one place he wanted to play, our family-owned team, Triple Twisters.

When Jenson and Chad retired from playing professional ball, they didn't want to give up the game altogether. Jenson is the head coach and Chad is the assistant. They were practically as excited as we were seeing as they helped train Huxley since back in his little league days.

"Grandma!" Mariella yells as Sara enters the room to join us. She hugs her as soon as she is within arm's reach.

With both sets of biological grandparents being deceased Sara took on the surrogate role of grandma to the kids.

As I look around the room and survey all the family and friends my heart is so full. I'm thankful every day for Jenny and the kids. Thankful that sixteen years ago a struggling single mom took me up on a wild hair-brain deal to temporarily marry me. Thankful that Jenny fell in love with me just as much as I fell for her and that she has remained a constant in my life.

Our love has only grown over the years despite all the hardships we've faced. We survived Carlos going to jail for his attack on Jenny. Survived the grueling court battle when Jenny petitioned for Carlos' parental rights to be terminated and I filed to adopt Rae and Huxley. We survived an unexpected and difficult pregnancy Jenny faced when birthing Mariella, which caused her to be temporarily hospitalized during the second trimester. We survived two of our kids flying the nest. Hopefully, we can once again survive the teenage years as Mariella continues to grow.

Looking back on it all, with Jenny by my side, not only did we survive but we thrived. Nothing could be sweeter than this life we built together.

About the Author

Savanna Golden is an author from the Midwest. When not spending time with her husband and five kids she can be found with a book in hand. Her favorite genres to read are romance and fantasy. Her favorite romance trope is enemies to lovers and her least favorite is tied between second chance and miscommunication.

Want to get social? Scan for all of Savanna's important links:

Also By

Love was the last thing on Finley's mind, especially after the heartbreak she faced a few years prior. But when her best friend urges her to try a dating app, Finley unexpectedly finds her fated mate, Alexander, a mischievous and charming warlock. Little did she know, their love would be tested when a new alpha takes leadership of her pack and threatens to tear them apart.

Finley and her band of misfit supernatural friends make it their mission to stop the tyrant and save her pack. With emotions running high and danger lurking around every corner, Finley must decide who to trust and how far she's willing to go for love.

If you enjoy steamy and fun fantasy romances set in the modern world, you won't be able to put down this book. Mate Match is likely to make you laugh, cry, get angry, and swoon as you follow Finley and Alexander's journey.